S

a Compilation of Short African-American Science Fiction and Flash Fiction

BIEN-AIMÈ WENDA

Illustrated by
NORVIANCE HENRY

with contributions by
Rich H.
&
Solace of Om

Cover Design by Tina Shrivers

To all
science-fiction lovers
everywhere
&
to my late father
Wilner Bien-Aime

CONTENTS

ACKNOWLEDGMENTS

I would like to thank first and foremost, the *Divine Greater Source. The All Knowing.* You've always been there for me. Secondly, my daughter for putting up with me always being busy with working and writing. Also, my late father who loved me so much and I, him. I also would like to thank my mom, Roselande Foreste, for passing down her great genes to me (she's a songwriter, having written over 40 songs!)

The following people I cannot thank enough: My cousin, (the chocolate vixen) Marlene Casimir, my blessed and highly favored, one-of-a-kind, beautiful & genuine friend with such a wonderful spirit, Brenda Pierre, and last but not least, the ONLY man who knows me like the back of his hand, Jeremy Edward Dennis. I love you guys for doing what you were never obligated to do: supporting and encouraging little ol *me* from day one.

I wouldn't feel right without also sending out a great big special THANK YOU to my WBAC family for lighting my fire. Also my illustrator *(who's also a writer by the way)* and my contributors (both brilliant poets): NorViance Henry, Rich H., and Solace of Om. I hope to work with all of you again very soon.

STAGNANT MAJIK

I

"Yo doc! He good to go?"

Some young cat, probably about 10 years younger than I was, with a blue hoodie, Timbs, and a fresh high-top fade was pointing directly at me. Who the fuck was this dude and didn't his peeps ever teach him that it was disrespectful to point? And where in the fuck was I? This was definitely not Sojourner Truth Hospital. This place looked like someone's messy ass attic or basement or some shit.

A fine, thick, Dominican-lookin' chick, with shoulder-length curls, dressed in a tight purple tank top with an amethyst stone dangling around her neck walked over to where I was laying. I became suddenly aware that there were tubes and wires connected to the middle of my forehead.

"How you doin'?" She asked me. *Wow*, shorty was even sexier up close. I couldn't speak, my mouth was too parched and my body felt too weak so I gave her a half smile.

"Hand me that cup over there, Freddie." She instructed, looking at the young dude standing at the foot of the bed, or whatever the fuck this was that I was laying naked on.

Oh shit, I'm naked! The fuck was I doing naked?

With the exception of my large sapphire ring on my right hand, I was as naked as the day I came into existence 29 years ago. I tried to ask the chick to bring me my clothes but couldn't. My mouth was parched and felt as if I hadn't brushed in ages. I tried to use my tongue to conjure up some spit but that shit only made it worse. Yeah, I was most definitely dehydrated and my throat was beginning to itch *bad*.

I lifted my left arm and used my hand to form a letter "C", then moved it towards my mouth in a drinking motion.

"Don't worry, we gotchu, bro. Don't speak." Her large hazel eyes twinkled as she laughed. *Damn, she had some sexy ass eyes.*

Young dude came back with a small shot-glass filled with water. I gave him a *what the fuck?* look. The fuck was I supposed to do with that? I wanted to tell him to go back and just bring me the whole got-damn gallon but I was thirsty as fuck, and at the moment, my mouth was yearning for even a droplet of *any* liquid.

"Remove the monitors from the pineal." The chick instructed and young dude quickly moved to my left and ripped out the cords taped onto the middle of my forehead. *Ouch*! I rubbed my forehead and felt the sticky residue of the adhesive from the tape. I was getting aggravated.

The chick was still carefully holding on to the shot glass wedged between her right thumb and index finger. Now that I was free from the cords, I tried to sit up and reach for the glass but couldn't move. My body was so fuckin weak!

She moved closer to me and spoke slowly. "Huey," *How did she know my name?* "What I'm about to say is going to sound very strange but I want you to try to follow the instructions ok?"

I nodded while I kept my eyes on the shot glass that was now only within an arm's reach. My throat was beginning to feel like it was closing in. *I hope these fools don't let me die.*

"Frederick, don't forget the chart." She reminded the young dude, still standing over to the left of my head. He bent down and swiftly came back up with a clipboard. "Make a note: 29-year-old male in great physical shape. Head full of healthy-looking locs; look to be about 6'2-6'3." Youn dude began scribbling away.

I'm 6'4. I thought to myself, annoyed.

"Make that 6'4." She corrected.

"Got it doc."

She began reading my vitals on the monitor that the cords on my forehead had been attached to as the boy took notes.

"Dimethyltryptamine level is on point. Antioxidant levels are even better. GMO have been completely removed. Lead and aluminum are also completely removed, *thank God.* Why did they ever start putting aluminum in deodorant anyway?" She shook her head. "Fluoride have also been completely flushed out. Magnesium levels are back to normal and most importantly, the gluten issue is gone and as a result, just like I thought, the early signs of lupus and heart disease have also vanished. We'll keep him on the protein plants as well as the superfood diet: kale, blueberries, walnuts," she instructed, mentally checking each one off with her finger as she recited each plant-based food, "Strawberries, watercress and...." She tapped her index finger on her chin as she tried to think.

"Chia and quinoa?" The young dude asked, reading notes on the clipboard.

She snapped her fingers. "That's right. I always forget those two."

I sighed in defeat. All that shit she just read and that dumb ass machine couldn't tell that I was about to die from dehydration?

As if she could read my thoughts, the chick finally looked directly at me. "Huey, I know you're thirsty. I'm going to ask you to do something really important for me. As I warned you before, it might sound really crazy but I need you to just try and do it okay?"

Jaws clenched, I stared at her, hoping she could read the frustration in my eyes.

She continued. "So, without getting up or using your arms, I need you to take this cup."

I scrunched up my forehead. *The fuck?*

Maaaan, where was my aunt Gladys? These fools were about to have me laid out on this table dead. I tried to reach for the glass but she swatted my hand away and took a step back. I looked at the young brother with a pleading look in my eyes, begging for mercy. That piece of shit had the nerve to look directly at me and then went to scribbling in his fuckin' clipboard again. I vowed with every fiber of my being to beat his ass if I survived this shit.

The chick snapped her fingers in front of me, steering my attention back to her. "Huey, how bad do you want this?" Her hazel eyes were partially hidden by the clear shot glass as she slowly moved the glass back and forth in front of her face.

This dumb bitch. I was raised to never call a woman out her name but this dumb broad here was playing with my damn life.

II

"Huey, use your mind to take the shot glass. I know it sounds crazy but you can do it. Just try. All you gotta do is try it one time. Just once. I promise I'll have Frederick bring you a whole gallon of fresh cold spring water. Deal?"

My eyes widened. Why the fuck didn't these numbnuts just bring out the whole gallon in the first doggone place? These people had to be from Florida. Everyone knew Floridians were backward ass people. I wanted to get this shit done and over with so I tuned everything out and concentrated my thoughts on that tiny glass. I tried to imagine the glass in my hand.

What the fuck?

Before I knew what was happening, that fucking shot glass was traveling in mid-air towards me! Mid-air! The glass! The fucking shot glass was traveling in mid-air!

My eyes felt like they were about to jump out the sockets and hi-five my eyebrows. I turned to look at the young dude in a panic and heard the cup drop to the ground with a *thud!*

"This is why we use plastic." She chuckled as she bent over to grab the cup.

What in the hell kinda voodoo shit was this? Wait, maybe I had been wrong. Maybe this bitch was Haitian.

"Look, you got one more time to call me a bitch." She threatened with her right eyebrow raised at me and left hand on her hip.

It was at that moment that my heart felt like it was plummeting down a long flight of stairs. This b-, this *chick* could read thoughts! My hope for survival went straight down the fuckin' drain.

III

I didn't know where I was or who these weird people were.

Shorty, can I please get a glass of water? I am thirsty! I pleaded in my thoughts. I was hoping I hadn't gone crazy and perhaps shorty really could read my mind. Shit, maybe I was delirious from a lack of H2o.

To my surprise and her amusement, the Dominican or possibly Haitian chick's contorted lips released a sexy smile, revealing a deep dimple buried in her left cheek. "Nah, don't worry, you're not going crazy." She chuck-led.

Where am I? Where's my aunt Gladys? Where am I?

Where was my mama, Grannie and my aunt Gladys? They would never let this go down like this if they knew what was going on. Especially my aunt Gladys. She was my mother's older sister but she'd practically raised me since I was born. She didn't have any kids of her own and we were more like mother and son then aunt and nephew.

"We found you laying on the side of a dirt road in Arizona. Do you remember that?" She asked.

Arizona? I'd never been to Arizona. I was born and raised in Inglewood, California. The last thing I could remember was heading out the house in search of some clean water. Grannie and mama had insisted that I take my pistol with me because....*Oh shit!*

"So it's all coming back to you now, good. Frederick and I were a little worried about you." She stated, walking over with a mini purple flashlight. She lifted my right eyelid and began blinding me with the beaming light. I shook my head from left to right uncooperatively. I wanted answers and I wanted them now.

Where's my mom, aunt, and grandma?

She flicked off the light and those beautiful eyes peered directly into mine. "Huey, I'll answer all of your questions in just a minute, but right now I need you to relax. We're only here to help. I need to make sure that your pineal gland is entirely decalcified before you're released." She tried to reassure me.

"Now let's try this again. Let's reattach the frequency monitors to the pineal gland. Freddie get me another cup, please. This time let's use one of the Styrofoam cups over there on top of the file cabinet."

I let my questions go for now as I felt my body become weaker. My main concern for the moment was getting hydrated. I needed to get well enough to find my family.

"Thank you, Freddie." She grabbed the plastic shot glass from young dude. "Alright, Huey, you ready? Let's try this again." She ordered with the cup sitting patiently on her right palm.

This time, with little effort, the cup immediately lifted off her palm and floated towards me. I lifted my smiling face in anticipation, not wanting the precious water to waste again. As soon as it was within arm's reach I snatched and held the Styrofoam cup up to my cracked lips. I leaned my head back and my throat felt like it was singing songs of praise at the feel of liquid. I had never before felt so happy to taste a swig of water in my entire life!

Freddie, the young dude, startled me when he spoke and grabbed the cup. I had forgotten that he was even there. I wondered if he could also read thoughts. "You should be able to speak now, dawg."

Frederick and the chick both stared at me as I cleared my throat. The way they were both looking at me made me feel like a new born baby about to speak his first words.

"Bring the whole gallon." I managed to whisper.

IV

The chick had made good on her promise. She brought over a whole gallon of cold alkaline water and I think I swallowed it all in one gulp.

Then I went the fuck off.

"Where the fuck is my mother, my grannie and my aunt? Take this shit off me!" I ripped off the fucking cords that were attached to my forehead and flung both legs over the makeshift bed.

I could tell that my sudden change in behavior had alarmed them both but I was enraged. Both the chick and young dude took a step back with their hands up in front of their chest, frightened, as if this were a stick-up.

"Where are my clothes?" I hopped off the bed and my knees buckled unexpectedly beneath me. How long had I been unconscious?

I held onto the bed like a toddler learning to walk as I began to question them. "I asked you a question! Who are you and where the fuck is my family?"

The chick spoke up first. She took in a deep breath then released it and took a step towards me.

"My name is Rosa. This is my younger brother Frederick." She pointed at Freddie who was still standing behind her with his hands up in front of him.

"Man, put your damn hands down." I ordered. Instead of complying, he took another step back with his hands still placed in front of him.

I looked at Rosa. "What's up with him and can a brother *please* get his clothes back or do I have to perform more magic tricks? And what the fuck was that all about a few second ago? What did you do to me? How'd I do that with the cup?"

"Frederick, go get Huey his clothes," Rosa ordered with an attitude while looking directly at me.

"And how do you know my name?" I added.

She answered calmly, "You are on the planet Negus. Your government and the elites, the puppet masters who ran the government, abandoned Earth to take residence on a super planet—"

"Oh you mean that planet they just discovered, Super Earth." I interrupted, taking everything she was saying with a grain of salt. The chick sounded crazy!

"I am not *crazy*!" She shouted irritably. She crossed her arms and pursed her full sexy lips.

"Could you please stop doing that?!" I shouted, referring to the lack of privacy I had within my own thoughts.

"You think I can just turn this shit off and on when I want?! Now do you wanna know where your family is or not? I got other shit I need to be doing right now." She snapped.

"I'm sorry, my bad, continue." I urged apologetically. This time I was the one raising both hands in surrender.

She didn't get a chance to continue as I went crashing down onto the hard-carpeted floor. I groaned and slightly lifted up my bottom to rub my tail bone. Rosa rushed over to me and grabbed one of my arms.

"Oh my god, Huey, are you okay? I think you should lay back down before you hurt yourself."

"Too late." I groaned.

She helped me onto the bed just as the boy was walking in. He handed Rosa some unfamiliar overalls and a plaid shirt.

"Those definitely aren't mine. I don't wear plaid and I definitely don't do overalls." I told her before she even thought about handing those hillbilly garbs over to me.

"It's not about what you want, it's all we have right now. We had to get rid of all of your things. With the exception of that sapphire ring you have on, everything else had to be burned. They were highly toxic with lead and fluoride. Most likely from the water used to wash clothes."

"Toxic?"

"I'll explain later. Just put these on." She shoved the clothes onto my lap.

"I'm only putting on these overalls. So y'all don't have any boxers or anything for me to put on underneath? Never mind." I said, peeping the look of impatience on her beautiful face.

She looked over at Frederick and he left the room again.

"Now, what were you saying about my family?"

V

"The former rulers of Earth abandoned all of you and somehow managed to leave with all of its natural resources. Apparently, this had been something they had been planning for centuries which explained the lack of interest in preserving the environment and wildlife. They had even thought to make clones of talented celebrities to program for their entertainment on the new planet."

"I had heard about somethin' like that from my cousin Carmichael. We used to tease him and called him Tinfoil for laughs. He was the family's conspiracy theorist. Always coming up with these crazy ass theories." I stated retrospectively.

"My brother and I once too lived on Earth. Luckily, we heeded the warnings and were brought to this planet before the catastrophe. Since the chaos, we've been making regular trips to Earth to help save as many people as possible. As I stated before, we had found you dehydrated, laying on the side of the road in Phoenix, AZ. We brought you back here and began hydrating you through an IV. We had to detox your pineal gland for 4 months to get it completely decalcified."

"Wait, *four months*?! My family must be worried sick about me! I was just supposed to be going out to search for water. *Oh my god*." I began to weep into my palms unashamedly.

Rosa placed a hand on my bare shoulder. "Huey, listen to me. We were able to find your mother and aunt. They're both fine and recuperating in the other room." She quickly reassured.

I breathed a sigh of relief. "What about grannie?"

She removed her hand from me and looked down.

My heart sank. "What? Did something happen to grannie?"

She finally made eye contact. "I'm sorry Huey. By the time we had gotten to her it was too late. The lack of hydration combined with the summer heat proved to be too much for her elderly body. I'm so sorry Huey, I promise you we did all that we could."

I fought back tears as I asked, "How long ago did you say this was?"

"Four months ago. As soon as we found you, I had Frederick use his pineal to read your past and find your loved ones. As soon as we made it to them, they had all just collapsed from dehydration but we were only able to save your aunt and your mom."

I didn't stop the tears from forming a river down my face as I stared absentmindedly at the ground. My grannie was gone. She was *gone*. Had I went to look for water earlier.....

"Huey, listen to me, *there was nothing you could have done to save her*. The planet of Earth was deteriorating at a rapid pace; it was intentionally depleted of all natural resources...including water. You would have been out searching in vain." Rosa grabbed my hand as she explained. "Is there anyone else back home that you would like for us to find? Any children? Wife?"

I shook my head sorrowfully. "We all thought my cousin Carmichael was crazy when he tried to tell us. We thought he'd lost it."

"Where is he? Shall we send out a search party to try to find him?" She asked.

"He mysteriously disappeared long before the chaos was even on the horizon. He had told me months before to stock up on clean water but I wouldn't listen and now grannie....." I broke down into a sob, no longer able to hold back the flood of emotions.

Rosa covered my body with hers as she embraced me. "I'm so sorry, Huey. I'm so sorry." She whispered.

We both stayed in this position for a minute or so. There was something about the touch of a woman during a time of trouble. Her touch and her scent, a mix of a coconut and vanilla aroma, were both very comforting to me.

"What happened to your family? Were you able to save them all?" I asked.

Her dark brown shoulder-length curls did a slow dance as she shook her head. "No. It's only me and Freddie. My parents refused to leave their home and all of their belongings when it was time to go. My religious sister and her husband were adamant that this was the apocalypse, which I guess in some ways you can say it was. They were convinced that the rapture would happen and wanted to stay on Earth."

"What happened to them? Are they still alive?"

She stared off in the distance and answered softly as tears formed in her eyes. "I haven't been able to bring myself to check. It's been 7 months and I can't bring myself to see them like that. I prefer to have my last memories of them alive and well and not as....... corpses."

"Rosa, I'm so sorry for your loss."

Rosa snapped back to the present. She shook her tears away and smiled at me. "It's ok. Since coming to Negus and having proven to everyone that my theory on 3rd eye restoration were indeed *factual*, I was designated as the planet's resident physician."

"Physician? And how old are you?" I asked skeptically. She had a baby face. She had to be no more than twenty-one.

"I'm twenty-six and you don't have to believe me. My strong intuition," She used her index finger to tap the middle of her forehead, her 3rd eye, "and my ability to read minds even while a patient is asleep or nonresponsive has helped thousands of people. The very fact that you're alive and well speaking to me should speak for itself, don't you think?"

I nodded apologetically. That would explain why the boy called her *doc*.

"Freddie is the only person I have not been able to fully restore back to the young vibrant teen that he was. His third eye work. He's healthy physically but mentally and emotionally, he's all fucked up. He rarely speaks or sleep. I'm afraid the type of doctor that he needs to see is one for the psyche. All of the recent events have taken a traumatic toll on him."

I nodded sympathetically, still unable to fully digest everything I'd just been told.

"Although the residents of Negus do not believe in a government-type system. We do have one leader but he's very kind and compassionate. In fact, he was the one who discovered this planet in this galaxy. Kwame has dedicated the majority of his adult life secretly locating a planet far away from the evil ones of the Milky Way."

Frederick walked in with what looked to be about 3 or 4 pairs of boxers folded neatly in his hands. "Kwame would like to speak with Huey."

Concern covered Rosa's light brown face "Did you tell him that the patient has not yet regained full use of both legs?"

"Yes, doc. He said he would speak to him here."

I'm not gonna lie, the look on Rosa's face had me a little nervous.

"Does he speak to every new person?" I asked her.

She shook her head. "No. This is a first but I guess there's a first time for everything, right?" She chuckled awkwardly.

"Should I be concerned?" I asked in a no-nonsense tone, immediately thinking of ways to defend myself despite the lack of full function of my legs.

The sound of Rosa's laughter literally sounded like music to my ears. "Don't worry, he's not that type of guy so whatever you're thinking, stop."

"He's coming." Frederick announced in a hushed whisper from in front of the doorway.

Rosa caught me by surprise with a quick peck on my cheeks. "You'll be fine." She reassured me with a flirtatious smirk.

She made her way towards her younger brother and wrapped her arm around his shoulder before exiting.

"Huey?" A tall man the color of pecan, with large thick dark reading glasses entered the room dressed in all white.

I squinted until he came closer. "Carmichael?"

He looked overcome by emotion. Tears were welling up in the corners of his eyes as he tried his best to smile. Carmichael looked genuinely pleased to see me.

"I go by Kwame now. I made them go look for you guys."

"Even after we ridiculed you?" I was full of remorse.

He nodded. "Hey, we're family. That's what we do."

"And grannie, did they tell you about grannie?" My voice shook and before I knew it, I was sobbing again.

Carmichael......Kwame used his body to envelope mine in a familiar tight embrace as we both wept for our grannie, for Earth, and for the state of humanity

KINDRED SPIRITS

A flash fiction

*"In a perfect world,
I'd remove the mask of pretense & perfection ...
To feel with every fiber of my being...to feel confident that the one chosen for me is genuine, and for him to examine and kiss my flaws and proclaim to the entire world: 'There's no place like home...there's no place like home...there's no place like HOME' "-Bien-Aimè Wenda*

"Sapphire."

He called for me, as if we weren't both laying side by side on the vibrant green grass along a babbling streaming brook, staring up at the bright blue sky. He passed me a joint and I inhaled it deeply. Gazing at the warm sky, I couldn't help but to chuckle. The sky seemed to also be smoking a joint, as the clouds resembled puffs of smoke.

I giggled uncontrollably.

"Sapphire." He called again.

He turned his thin lanky body over to his side and commenced using his smooth wide espresso-toned nose to nestle his way past my braids to find my neck, all the while using his long arms to cuff my waist in a tight grip.

"Hmm?" I answered without opening my mouth, not wanting to release the smoke I was holding inside.

"I love you." He planted a wet kiss on my round cheek.

"And I, you, Amethyst."

Carefully holding the joint between my left index finger and thumb, I rolled my pudgy cinnamon colored frame to my right to face my beautiful kindred spirit.

Our lips interlocked.

Our tongues played a quick game of tag.

I giggled, ending the tease.

Taking one last puff before snuffing out the joint and laying it beside me on the grass, I gave my twin flame my undivided attention. Running my short fingers through the manifestation of patience that was Amethyst's long dark locs, the hummingbirds in the distance serenaded us with a beautiful love song.

Amethyst kissed a delicate spot on my shoulder. "Promise you'll never leave me, babe."

My right hand grabbed his left hand and our fingers intertwined, the sapphire stones on his wedding band exposed; a reminder of the vows we had spoken in the presence of only our immediate family and close friends two summers ago, in Honolulu. We both stared intensely at the beautiful embrace of his expresso-colored fingers between my own cinnamon-toned skin.

"Til death do us part, baby." I said.

"I mean it. Even after death; in the next lifetime and the lifetime after. Promise we'll find each other always and fall in love all over again." He requested softly.

I chuckled bashfully although my heart felt like it had just melted into a large rippled puddle of love.

"I promise." I vowed as our lips connected for an encore.

"Excuse me, queen, don't I know you from somewhere?"

I crinkled my nose as if I had just stepped on a pile of dog shit. Why was this average-lookin' nigga tryin' to talk to me? I felt offended that he even thought that he had a chance with *me*.

Giving him another once-over, it was clear that we were definitely *NOT* in the same league. For one, he stood a lot shorter than my slender five foot nine frame. Not only was he rocking some tired ass old-school cornrows, but compared to my designer clothing, he looked like a straight-up bum in his off-brand gear. To top that off, he was also overweight. Short and fat were definitely a bad combination. Him even standing in my presence attempting to get my digits was just an overall bad look for me, *period*. There was no way that he was in his right mind when he had decided to walk from the other side of the gift shop to try to get my number. Who the hell does that?

Secondly, we were at fucking Walt Disney World for chrissake! More than likely, we were both tourists and lived in completely different states. I wasn't even attracted to him *anyway*, so even if we *had* lived in the same city, it wouldn't have even mattered. The sight of him repulsed me.

I glanced around the gift shop to see who the hell he had come in with. I wanted to see who had encouraged this fool and puffed him up enough to believe that he actually had a shot with *me*?

I sighed. "Sorry, but I gotta man." I lied, giving myself a pat on the back for being nice enough to shoot him a phony smile.

He pushed his fat stubby nubs for fingers into his oversized jean pockets and looked down, obviously disappointed.

Just as he was about to finally turn to leave from my presence, he pointed at the amethyst necklace around my neck. "Look at that, we got matching chains."

Out of habit, my thumb and index fingers rubbed over the purple amethyst stone hanging from an 18-karate roped-style chain.

"See? Look at mine." He pulled out a cheap looking thin-linked chain hiding underneath his dated Chicago Bulls jersey. What was he talking about?

Our necklaces look nothing alike, I thought, as he held up a sapphire ring dangling on the cheap chain around his neck.

I was suddenly overcome with a sense of deja-vu; an eery feeling of familiarity washing over me, as if I'd known this man from somewhere.

It frightened me.

"It's a sapphire." He stated.

"I know what it is." I said, this time letting my annoyance out on full display.

"I'm Aaron. What's your name?" He extended a chubby hand towards me.

Feeling like this conversation had went way over its time limit, I looked around the large gift shop. "I gotta go. My man waitin' for me outside." I lied again, leaving the groundhog-lookin' dwarf standing by the shelves of Disney DVDs.

An underlying feeling of sadness caught me by surprise as I laughed to myself. At the age of 29, I couldn't even remember the last time I had a real man. One who I had actually felt a real connection with. In fact, I don't think I had ever had that; but nevertheless, I was still hopeful.

I knew that one day I would run into my kindred spirit.

SLEEPING GIANTS
(PART 1)

A flash fiction

"Still they knock?
To subside our homes?
Acting toward our doorstep
Cynical tapping against the door,
hoping to wine and dine within walls of this unity with
tales of divide and conquer." -Solace of Om

"Look at these idiots."

Two reptilians stood in front of a large monitor cackling as they watched the 10'o clock news. There was a celebratory feeling in the air as Zeke, the father of the younger reptile turned up the volume. They hung onto every word of the middle-aged African-American woman on the screen.

"The president has not yet spoken on the many protests taking place today. Several church leaders of the African-American as well as the Hispanic community have held press conferences asking members of the community to remain calm during these times of uncertainty."

Zeke clicked off the monitor and the object disappeared from thin air.

"Well father, seems like everything is going as planned. Full pandemonium. Citizens against police officers, black against white, Christians against Muslims, and even the straight against the gays. This was *genius*!"

"I told you, didn't I? Now all we do is sit back and wait for them to wipe each other off the planet so that our species can reign."

Argon, the younger reptilian, jumped up and down in excitement, his long scaly thin green tail whipping back and forth rapidly behind him. His father gave him a disapproving look.

"Hey, I still want you to continue rounding up the rest of the demons and using your disguises to fool the masses. We need more negative media out there. We need more division! More fear! Keep their frequency and vibrations low. Remember we can only use and control their minds and bodies if their frequency is low." He ordered sternly.

Argon nodded. "Mass deception. Smoke and mirrors. High frequency is our kryptonite."

Zeke rubbed his scaly green palms together with anticipation as he sneered. "*Excellent.*"

THE CHILDREN OF INDIGO

A flash fiction

Golden tiny, shiny things shimmering across these windows
Curtains open, eyes open...
Reflection...
Light embracing, light pervading body spirit and mind.
Why I feel fine inside
I feel light inside
I am light inside- Solace of Om

"Onyx, Topaz, Tourmaline, and Tiger Eye, you four stay seated right where you are. You won't be leaving as of yet." Rose-Quartz, or *Mother Nature*, as the children referred to her, instructed.

She continued. "Jade, Opal, Jasper, and Malachite, you four stand over here by the blackboard."

"Yes mother." They all responded in unison.

Rose-Quartz stood in front of the latter group. She beamed with pride as she stared down at them, causing her whole body to illuminate with a soft pink glow as she did so. Opal, Jade, Jasper, and Malachite stood side by side as they waited patiently for further instructions.

"Do you each remember all of your assigned tasks?" She queried while pacing back and forth in front of the children.

They all nodded eagerly.

"Malachite?" Mother Nature stopped directly in front of him, blocking his view of the other Indigo Children that were seated.

"Yes mother." Malachite answered courteously.

"Can you remind me of what your assigned task is?" She interrogated.

Malachite's entire body illuminated in a bright emerald green color as he answered, "To bring awareness to the importance of love for nature and the environment in an attempt to bring transformation to the earth. "

"Good job Malachite! You let them know that I was gracious enough to let them use my natural resources so they had better learn to take care of it." She warned.

Malachite nodded. "Yes, mother. I'll remember to do so."

Mother Nature smiled. "You may go."

She stepped aside and allowed the child to pass just as the white carpeted floor opened up to form a small circular tunnel. Malachite, smiling as he skipped to the hole, waved to all the other Indigo Children before sliding down the tunnel, also known as the birthing tunnel or simply, the birth canal. Just as quickly as it had opened, the hole on the ground closed shut and went back to camouflaging its existence under the white carpeted floor.

"Jasper you're up next. Do you remember your assigned mission as a Child of Indigo?" Rose-Quartz asked, her soft pink body flickering with illumination as she waited.

Jasper immediately floated in the air, causing the energy in the room to surge tremendously as his inner red light shone brightly. "Yes, mother. To help bring calm and relaxation during a time of trouble, by raising the vibration and demonstrating the power of love and meditation." He answered confidently.

Rose-Quartz body glowed as she nodded with pride. "You're free to go."

The ground opened up once again, revealing the tunnel as Jasper floated to it. He raised his hand to his temple to give Mother Nature a quick salute before allowing his body to drop down the birth canal.

As the tunnel moved to close again, Mother Nature ordered, "Remain open." In turn, the tunnel ceased all movement.

Mother Nature smiled as she walked towards Jade. "You ready Jade?"

Jade's inner soft light flickered green as she nodded in response.

"We both know you have a very challenging task ahead of you and I know you'll make us proud. Don't be afraid to use your gifts. It'll cause many to be uncomfortable and more than likely you will be a loner the majority of your youth but once you become of age, you will form friendships with other Indigo Children and your true power will manifest. Now go out there and show humanity how to love. Go heal the sick. Give generously. Raise the vibration. Make us proud."

Jade nodded humbly and walked to the tunnel. Without as much as a goodbye wave, she immediately slid down the tunnel, knowing that time was of the essence. There was far too much work to be done to restore the state of humanity.

"Ahh, last but certainly not least, my Opal." She stared at the young female child with adoration. The small child smiled back timidly.

"This is going to be your greatest challenge yet because it'll require you to break out of that shyness and display your uniqueness. Like Jade, your assignment is also imperative to the restoration of society, and just like Jade, you will have a bigger workload than the rest. Do you understand your assigned tasks?"

Opal bent her head towards the ground as she nodded timidly. "To create?" She whispered inquisitively.

"Go on." Mother Nature urged warmly.

Opal clasped her hands behind her back as slid her right foot from side to side nervously, as if drawing an imaginary line. "To encourage others to tap into their creativity and to inspire others." She finally looked up at Mother Nature, waiting for approval.

"And do you remember *why* this is an important assignment?"

She nodded. "Because I will have to intermittently remind the other Indigo Children to make use of their gifts."

Overfilled with love and joy, Rose-Quartz tried to keep a professional disposition but her pink glow was shining throughout the room.

"Yes, my dear child. So it's important that you break out of that shyness and fear of what others will think of you. You have to also remind the others to let go of the fear of failure. For there is no such thing as failure when it comes to creativity. Always remind the others: the courage of beginning the creative process is in itself a victory and the beginning of a series of other victories. Got that?"

Opal nodded eagerly.

"You're free to go. "She gently pushed Opal towards the tunnel. "Make me proud, Opal, for I know it's within you. Go out there and remind the rest of the Indigo Children to promote love within the world through the use of their creative gifts."

And with that, Mother Nature and the remaining seated Indigo Children all cheered as Opal slid down the birthing canal with purpose.

THE AFTER-LIFE

I

When I was ten, my dad installed 3 double bolt locks in every door that led to the outside world. Almost every night, like clockwork, I would get up from my bed to take a journey outside. Of course, I could never remember any of it the next morning and I would always beg my parents to wake me up whenever they caught me in the act. They refused. Ten was the age I had started sleepwalking.

The sleeping walking episode only lasted until I was about twelve and had never returned.

Or so I thought.

I was wondering if it had suddenly decided to make a reappearance at age 20, because I was suddenly somewhere I hadn't remembered driving or walking to. This place didn't seem familiar to me at all and I couldn't remember how I had gotten here.

Somehow, I was standing inside of what could only be described as a never-ending bright room with blinking lights. There had to be at least a million and one flickering blue lights directly on the white walls. There was not one space of wall that did not have blinking lights. Where the hell was I? Had the breakup finally caused me to go completely mad?

"Deidre? This isn't funny Deidre!" An alarm sounded throughout my whole body when I heard no answer.

I took a step forward from the center of the room and squinted, my eyes attempting to readjust to the brightness. I needed to be able to see if someone or *something* jumped out at me. I forced myself to take in a deep breath and tried slowing down my heart rate just enough to be able to think clearly. With my hands cupped over my mouth, I spoke. "MOM? DAD?"

No answer.

Something caused me to look down. Perhaps it was the fact that I was barefoot and the ground seemed to be not only a bright white color but I felt like I was walking on soft cotton. Instinctively, I crouched down to touch the ground and I watched as my hand pushed through the soft cloud-like surface. I nearly jumped back in horror when I realized that my hands were unrecognizable These hands lacked color. My real hands were a golden honey. They weren't white hands or brown hands. They were void of *any* color. Transparent; as in *see-through.* They were as clear as colorless wine glasses and the only thing I could see was the brown outline of my hand. I resembled a drawing that hadn't yet been colored in.

"Is this heaven?"

Perhaps I was still dreaming. I looked up and came to the conclusion that I *had* to be still dreaming because the room had no ceiling. But that wasn't what had me in awe. It was the fact that the scenery overhead resembled something straight out of an astronomy book.

Sparkling like a million miniature diamonds were a million little stars, somehow defying gravity and held up in the atmosphere in what looked to be a galaxy.

This wasn't a dream. This felt too real.

I shut my eyes and reopened them.

Dammit! I was still here.

I was also aware of my heightened senses as I felt and *heard* my heart return to thumping wildly inside my chest. My forehead crinkled as I desperately tried recalling the exact details of the last thing I had been doing before whatever had just happened, happened.

"WAKE UP!" I tried yelling to my sleeping self, hoping to awaken in a room of familiarity.

"WAKE UP, FREIDA!"

This time with as much force as I could possibly muster, I extended my right hand as far back as I could, then brought it forward to connect with my cheek in a powerful SLAP! I rubbed my cheekbone, cringing from the tingling sting of my own attack.

Off to my right, I heard a snicker.

I spun around and discovered a teenaged girl staring at me in amusement. Her head was crowned with a small black afro. Like me, she was also void of color with the exception of a dark chocolate outline.

2

"Virtue, that's not nice." A male voiced boomed overheard, reprimanding sternly but gently.

I jumped and tried to locate the owner of the voice but saw no one else.

The young woman pouted, "But she did it to me yesterday. You guys are always taking her side."

Another woman appeared from out of nowhere; or perhaps she had been there the whole time? She had striking beautiful lavender-colored pupils. Her outline was the color of a light brown ginger root and her hair fell in a bundle of golden peanut butter-colored locs down to her waist. She walked towards the girl and placed both hands on her hips. She stood about an inch or two taller than the girl.

"Virtue, you know she's gonna get you back right?" The woman laughed, "Her memory should be kickin' in soon so we need to hurry. I only have about 15 more minutes to get her over to the advising room." She announced.

She then used those lavender eyes to look directly at me. Startled, my flight-or-fight instincts finally kicked in. I cautiously took a step back......away from the both of them.

"Get away from me!" I warned.

The woman took a step forward, her right hand stretched out towards me, "We're not going to hurt you."

Looking around the bright room and flickering lights I commanded the woman, "Take me off of this.... this......this *spaceship* and bring me home! NOW!"

"Spaceship?" Virtue, the teenaged girl, was beginning to aggravate me as she held her stomach and hunched over in a fit of giggles, ignoring the urgency in my voice.

I looked directly at her as I sneered, "Where's the captain? I need to speak to the leader of this ship at once! My father is a very powerful attorney and once he realizes that I've been kidnapped, the whole United States military will be on all of your asses!"

Virtue finally stopped laughing and shook her head at me. "Your *father*, is not a powerful attorney. He's just a typical small-town lawyer and as far as the military is concerned, there would be no need to call on them because your body isn't missing, it's still laying on Deidre's shabby bed, with dried tear stains on your face from crying over that pathetic human boy-"

"Virtue! Enough!" The woman with the golden locs snapped.

"What is she talking about? Take me home! RIGHT NOW!"

Virtue huffed and took a step towards me. "*YOU'RE DEAD, STUPID!*" She impatiently revealed.

3

"Dead?" I repeated.

"*Yes, dead!* As of 2:59 am this morning, mortal time of course, you've been dead; stiff as a board." Said Virtue.

My knees buckled. "This can't be. Oh my God! Deidre! My parents! And Terrell.... I have to talk to him. I need closure. I must go back at once!" I demanded, as I remembered the people who meant the most to me back home.

***

"Forget him Free, you don't need his sorry tail anyway." Deidre tried her best to console me, just as a best friend should.

I continued staring straight ahead, numb. She locked her arm with mine and we both sat in silence on her queen-sized canopy bed. I sniffed and let my thoughts torture me as I used a fistful of balled up Kleenex to catch a persistent slime of snot attempting to slide onto my lips. These same lips that Terrell had been kissing and biting on just four days ago. He had often told me how much he loved my full lips. In fact, physically speaking, I was every man's dream woman: 5 foot 9, curvy, vibrant caramel skin, light brown eyes, long dark hair that flowed past my shoulders, and pretty feet. In addition, I was also about to receive my degree in Communication in just two days and had been on the verge of signing a major publishing contract that my father was supposed to be looking over. I had written a sci-fi series year ago and had been ecstatic about finally getting it published.

The fact that Terrell had left me for a portly woman more than triple my size boggled my mind. The fact that he had the balls to admit to the infidelity just days before my graduation party via *text message* left me wondering if he had ever truly loved me.

Deidre was right, I didn't need him but I did *want* him. I loved and had fallen hard for him since the night we had met at an urban poetry spot on East Las Olas Blvd. I had just gotten off the stage from reading a poem when Deidre had called me right after my performance to tell me that she wouldn't be able to make it. As usual, her beat up '95 Ford escort was acting up again. Not in the mood to stick around the poetry lounge alone, I grabbed my coat to leave until I heard the sexiest baritone from behind me.

"Leaving already?" The voice was rich, confident and deep; and although I was sure that whoever it was wasn't speaking to me, I turned around anyway, curious to see who owned such a sensually masculine voice.

I lost my footing, making a complete fool out of myself, when I took in the Adonis standing before me. He was speaking to *me*.

"You okay?" He asked, the reflection of the stage lights twinkling in his dark brown eyes. Unable to speak, I nodded.

The brother was *FINE*. He was towering over me, so I figured he had to be between 6 feet and 6'2. Me being taller than the average woman, I loved taller men. He also looked like a poet himself with his unruly, nonconforming mini 'fro and goatee. He looked smooth in black jeans, a tan turtleneck, and a thin black chain with an amethyst pendant adorning his chest.

"I loved your piece. I kinda been checking you out since I started frequenting this joint. Finally got the courage to speak so please be easy on me." He chuckled nervously and that relaxed me.

I looked up to make eye contact and gave him my friendliest smile. "Well I was about to leave but I guess I can hang around for just a few more minutes. Have a seat."

And that began the commencement of our 4-year relationship.

Terrell Watson had been a very sweet and considerate boyfriend and not only was he a great lover, he was also gifted in the art of mental stimulation. He knew how to make a woman feel special, like she was all that mattered in his world. Many times I arrived to his place after enjoying a romantic dinner date or cozy boat ride, did I find rose petals strewn strategically on his black plush carpet leading into the bedroom.

Yes, things hadn't been going well for the past 6 months but that was due to my studies, internship and work life. It wasn't my fault. I had to have my priorities in order as a senior. I no longer had time to waste lounging around at his place. With Terrell being a Morehouse graduate, I assumed he would have understood. Instead he chose to rip my heart out my chest through a fucking *text*.

FREE, I CNT DO THIS N E MORE. YOU DSRV MORE THAN FOR ME TO TELL U THIS WAY BUT URE ALWYS TOO BUSY. 10:00PM

WHAT R YOU TLKIN ABOUT, TERRELL? 10:10pm

My voice finally shattered the memory, sending me back to the present as I thought out loud. "What is it that she has that I don't have? Why her? She doesn't even have a degree or anything going for her. She's not even all that *attractive*."

I could have cut the tension in Deidre's voice with a plastic knife as she answered, "Well, believe it or not, not all men care about degrees or *looks*. You can be as fine as Beyoncé and as smart as Michelle Obama and still be an undesirable woman." She unwrapped her arm from mine.

"You know I didn't mean it that way, right? I'm just-"

She put her hand up to stop me from continuing. "Say no more. I understand. You're not yourself right now."

I had forgotten about how self-conscious Deidre was about her weight ever since she had become a victim of the "Freshman 15" 4 years so. That is, the infamous 15 pounds that most students gained during their first year away at college. I felt like shit. Especially after remembering how she had generously offered for me to crash at her place for the past two days. I still lived at home with my parents' and couldn't bear the thought of being at home to cry alone, pretending everything was okay whenever my mom and pops stuck their head in my bed room.

IM SORRY, CN U PLZ PCK UP THE PHNE SO WE CN TLK 10:15pm

GO TO HELL TERRELL!!!! 10:19pm

Deidre continued, "Like I said, fuck Terrell. We need to be out looking for cute shoes and a nice outfit to wear with your cap and gown. So get your ass up, shower and get dressed."

4

I tried to feel normal during our excursion at the Oak Hill Mall, but the detox stage of healing from a break up had numbness taking complete control over my body. The smiles, the small talk, the laughter...they were all forced. Terrell was gone and he was all my thoughts wanted to obsess over.

In fact, my mind tortured me every day nonstop. Replaying the exact moment of devastation, as if on repeat.

FREE, I CAN'T DO THIS ANYMORE. YOU DESERVE MORE THAN FOR ME TO TELL U THIS WAY BUT URE ALWAYS TOO BUSY. 10:08pm

WHAT R U TLKIN ABOUT, TERRELL 10:10pm

IVE BEEN SEEING SHANNON. SHES PRGNANT. 10:11pm

UR EX???? 10:11pm

IM SORRY, CN U PLZ PCK UP THE PHNE SO WE CN TLK 10:15pm

GO TO HELL TERRELL!!!! 10:19pm

WILL U PLZ PICK UP THE PHNE FREE? 10:28pm

STOP CALLING MY FUCKIN PHONE!! 10:30pm

FRIEDA PLZ ANSWR THE DOOR 11:45pm

I was happy when Deidre and I had finally arrived back at her place.

"You alright Free?" I hadn't noticed Deidre standing behind me in her kitchen with both her hands on her hips, watching me stare absentmindedly into the open refrigerator. How long had I had been peering into the fridge? I shut the refrigerator door

"Yeah, I'm ok. Just tired. I think I'm gonna go shower now and call it a night. Do you mind if I crash here?"

"I'm not even gonna answer that. You know my place is your place."

For the first time that day I genuinely smiled in gratitude. I walked up to Deidre with outstretched arms and she rolled her eyes jokingly.

"Give me a hug." I said and wrapped my arms around her heavy frame. "I love you, I want you to always remember that."

She gave me a hug back before pushing me away. "Alright, alright, enough with the mushy stuff. Where did that come from?"

"What? I just wanted to give you a hug cus you're the bestest bestie a bestie could ever have as a bestie, bestie." I teased, clinging on to her as I gave her another tight hug.

"No, what I meant was, why did you tell me to always remember that? That was such an eerie thing to say."

It was my turn to roll my eyes. "Oh hush. I think I'm gonna call it a night. But first, I hear a nice hot bath calling me." I laughed as I walked past her towards the bathroom, intent on taking a much-needed long lavender bubble bath.

5

"Deidre has yet to discover your lifeless body. She goes jogging, shower and then heads directly to work on Wednesdays, remember? But don't worry, she'll eventually walk into her guest bedroom at around six p.m. after not hearing from you all day. They'll try to rule it as a suicide after finding booze and alcohol in your system." Virtue smiled, "It went just as you planned. You said you wanted to try a new exit, remember?"

The woman with the golden locs crossed her arms as she spoke, "You know she doesn't remember and next time you come back, I'm not gonna stop her from scaring you." She told the girl.

Filled with confusion and frustration, I wanted to cry but my eyes would not produce any tears.

Paralyzed with fear, my lips felt glued together as I watched Goldie Locs make her way toward me.

"Come on, time to complete the exit interview before the effects wear off."

I shouted as loud as I could, "WAKE UP! COME ON, WAKE UP!"

My eyes widened as the woman grabbed my wrist and led me out of the room of flickering lights.

/

6

"I just wanna go hooome." I whimpered, thinking of my mom, my dad, Deidre, Terrell and strangely even *Shannon*.

We walked through another room towards another door. Unlike the other room of flickering lights, this room was not as bright and had no flickering lights. Me being an avid reader, I was in awe at the number of bookshelves lining against the never-ending walls. There had to be *million* upon *millions* of books. In the middle of the room were about 200 colorless "beings" sitting in groups of four on the floor, seemingly comparing notes and scribbling in red notebooks.

"Whaddup Patience, back already?" Once of the male beings asked, looking directly at us. I noticed he was wearing one of those white karate-type attire. I looked down and noticed that I was also wearing the same gear.

I looked at the woman with the golden locs waiting for her to answer him.

She didn't. *That was rude.*

Patience? Her name didn't seem to fit her, although she had been very patient with me.

"Yo, Patience? It's me, Kindness." He reminded.

"He's talking to you." The woman with the golden locs specified.

I crumpled my forehead, "Me? But my name's F-"

"Here we are." Goldie locs interrupted as she led me to our destination; a brightly lit classroom filled with about 30 clear desks and a clear see-through podium at the front of the room. From behind the podium stood a tall male being with a beautiful outline of an array of colors. From black to pink to purple and there were even some breathtakingly beautiful colors that I had never seen before. He held a clip board and with the same booming voice I had heard overhead minutes ago, he greeted me.

"Welcome back, Patience." His voice was even more intimidating in person.

Again, I felt like I should be crying but for some reason, I couldn't. The being smiled and reassured with a look of genuine sincerity, "Don't worry, It's okay, we're not gonna harm you."

He looked at the woman still holding my now trembling hands. "Thank you, Passion. You may leave now."

I didn't want her leaving me here with this strange creature. "Wait!"

She stopped in her tracks and her long golden locs swayed as she turned to face me, eyebrow raised.

"Does Passion have to leave? I-- "

He interrupted as if he'd heard this a million times before. "She can't stay. Confidentiality reasons."

He nodded his beautiful outlined head towards her, signaling it was okay for her to leave. He waited until she made her exit before opening a manila folder on his clipboard.

"My name is Respect-"

"Respect?" I repeated as if he were insane.

He smiled. "I need you to answer some questions about your recent experience before your memory returns."

"Where am I?"

"You're home." He smiled.

7

"Home?"

"Yes. "

"What do you mean home? Take me home right this minute! I need to go home. I'm a day away from signing my contract for a book deal and a few days away from graduating college! I need to go back! Are you listening to me?!" I panicked.

Instead of responding, he calmly scribbled inside his manila folder.

"Calm down, Patience and take a deep breath. Go on, breathe."

I took in several deep breaths. "Look, I think you guys got the wrong person. My name's *Free*. It's short for Freida." I corrected.

"You'll be back in a human body tomorrow." He said and I breathed a sigh of relief.

"Okay *Frieda*, tell me, did you enjoy the experience? Tell me about the experience and the memories as a mortal. Although we did watch over you on the monitor, as a precaution of course, I still need to ask you some questions that you wanted answered."

"What? I'm sorry I'm a bit confused."

"Yes, I'm gonna try to make this as quick as possible, as time is of the essence and we only have a few minutes left. Before your journey to the realm in which you've just returned, you compiled a list of questions you requested that we ask you. You knew, as we all know, that the memory would wear off and although we do have the visual of your mortal life recorded, it's the *emotions*, the *frequency*, that you wanted answers to. You've earned your current name of Patience, but like us all, you have been going back to the mortal realm in hopes of climbing the ladder to earn the final rank of Love."

"Love?" I repeated. This was getting to be too much to take in.

"Yes, self-love and love for others. For as we all know, that's all that truly matters in the journey, remember?"

"That's right, love for self and others is the ultimate goal." I repeated. What was I saying? How did I know that? I began to feel a faint sense of déjà vu.

"Alright we need to make this quick." Respect stated. He kept his head down as he quickly asked, "Describe heartbreak. Is it the same as a feeling of betrayal?"

"Heartbreak?" I thought of Terrell and Shannon. I didn't want to answer but something in me, perhaps my higher sense of consciousness, urged me to answer quickly.

"It's the worse feeling you could ever imagine. It's unexpected, hurtful, and depressing. It causes you not to trust others completely, as the hurt is usually performed by the ones you love the most." I answered articulately, surprising myself.

"What about sex? Describe the feeling of an orgasm." Respect asked, his head still down. His writing utensil still scribbling away.

"An orgasm?" I asked, slightly embarrassed. There was no way I was answering that.

Sensing my hesitancy, he moved on to the next question on the list. "Describe jealousy. Make it quick, we don't have much time left." He rushed, scribbling furiously.

I quickly explained, "Jealousy is a negative feeling of desire for something you wish to have that someone else---"

"We know the definition, *describe* the emotion."

I thought hard. "Well, uhh.. jealousy is...is...."

My mind was suddenly drawing a complete blank. "Why can't I remember?"

"I don't feel so good." I groaned. I suddenly felt like I was being attacked with a dozen prickly thumb tacks.

"Don't fret, it's just your higher consciousness pushing through to take over. I'm afraid our time is up now." He explained with a look of sheer disappointment.

"*Whoa!* I can see you in color!" As if someone had decided to finally color us in, I was also able to see faint colors on the being as well as my own body beginning to fill in. The outline that previously displayed his colors had done no justice. With his body fully "colored in", he looked absolutely stunning as his skin sparkled with various colors.

"*Wow!*" I marveled at my skin's golden honey color. I could actually see golden specks of dust shimmering on my skin. I was actually shining like *gold!*

8

"Patience........is that you?"

Respect, my mentor and very attractive advisor was peering strangely at me with his royal blue eyes. I wanted to reach out and stroke his long locs, as I had often imagined doing so since being assigned as his apprentice. I should also mention that it was no small feat to be assigned to Respect. One had to be an advanced trekker, and that I was.

I nodded and smiled, although I felt a bit anxious. "So, how'd I do?" I held up my hands near my chest, both index and middle fingers crossed in anticipation.

He sighed in disappointment. "I was only able to get you to answer one damn question."

My mouthed dropped open. "*One*?"

"Yo, you were a tough cookie this time. Don't worry, there's always tomorrow."

"True." I agreed, my ego feeling a little deflated.

I had written twenty-six detailed questions that I needed answers to in order to be promoted to the next rank. However, I thought of the bright side: the longer I stayed on the rank of Patience, the longer I would have to work with my beautiful and admirable sensei, Respect. He had successfully achieved each rank and was given the opportunity to choose his new name. I already knew which name I would choose for myself once I became a sensei. *Destiny.*

Or maybe Honesty.

Nah, I liked Destiny.

Respect continued, "You know, you don't have to keep going back to back. You can rest a bit between voyages."

I gave him an incredulous look. "You know my motto, *no rest until the work is done.* I'll take a break once I reach my new level. And anyway, the voyage is only a day long."

It was true. A lifetime as a mortal equated to only a one-day journey away from home. So each day before leaving, I would draft my life plan, my purpose and my exit. Of course, once I transformed into a mortal, I would have no recollection of this and would have to figure it out on my own. The only clues I would have to go by would be intuition.

This go round as *Frieda*, I had opted for a life plan of an aspiring writer. Since my mission was to understand compassion and different emotions, I figured what better way to do that than to be a writer. I chose a drug and alcohol overdose as my exit just to add a little drama and excitement. I could have also chosen to exit at an older age but they say your work becomes acclaimed once you're deceased, so more than likely, during my next mission, *Frieda* will have been remembered as a writer extraordinaire.

There was an unexpected knock on the door.

"Come in." Respect answered and in walked a member of my family unit from a past life.

9

"Welcome back Patience!" My sister from a recent past life rushed toward me to give me a hug.

For some reason, after having to experience a mortal mother intentionally drowning us in a river, we had bonded and gotten even closer once we had arrived back home. Perhaps it was because the experience had been so traumatic as 4-year-old twins.

"Will you cut it out, you act like you didn't just see me yesterday, Virtue." I say but I can't help but to be amused. I know she's getting ready to give me the dirt.

"Girrrrl, you were acting a straight *DONKEY* this time! Slappin' yourself and all!" Virtue gushed, no doubt excited to be able to be the one to relay this information. Respect, who was usually pretty serious, surprised me when he let out a chuckle in agreement.

"Damn I was that bad? I hope you didn't do or say anything to scare me."

Knowing Virtue, she probably did and more than likely, that's probably why I hadn't had enough time to complete my exit interview. But it was cool, we always waited until the countdown of each other's return and made sure we were the first person each other seen; just to mess around.

"Yeah. I'm about to get ready to leave in a few. Guess what my exit will be?" She asked.

"Police shoot-out?"

She smiled. "Nope."

"Hmmm, drowning?"

"Hell no, I'm done with water deaths. Something exciting." She hinted, her eyes bulging the whole time.

"I already said police shoot out."

She finally gave in and by this time even Respect had a curious look on his face. "This time I'm going back as a world-famous gymnast. And my exit will be in front of a live audience. I'm gonna fall off a trapeze."

My mouth fell open. From the corner of my eye, I could see my sensei shaking his head in amusement.

There was another knock on the door, although the door was still ajar.

Compassion, our sweet designated entry and exit hostess, who was usually always in a rush to and from the birthing room, walked in and I greeted her.

"Hey Passion. I heard I was actin a straight fool this time."

"*Well.....*" She smiled politely.

I interrupted, laughing. "Say no more. I'll be reviewing the recordings shortly and I don't want anyone to spoil it for me."

"Trust me, I had no intentions on doing so. I came to tell Virtue her tunnel was ready." She looked at Virtue. "Come on, Virtue, let's get a move on. You can chat with Patience tomorrow when you get back."

"I'll walk you there." I quickly chimed, swinging my arm around Virtue's shoulder.

Passion, Virtue and I made our way back towards the birthing room, leaving Respect behind in the advising room.

When we finally made it to the birthing chamber, the indicator lights were already flickering yellow, signaling it was almost ready for take-off. We had made it just in time. The flickering lights switched to green, indicating the tunnel was about to make its appearance.

And that it did.

The soft puffy ground opened up in in the shape of a large black circle, ready for its participant to slide down. Sliding down the birth canal was always the fun part of the entire mortal experience, at least in my opinion.

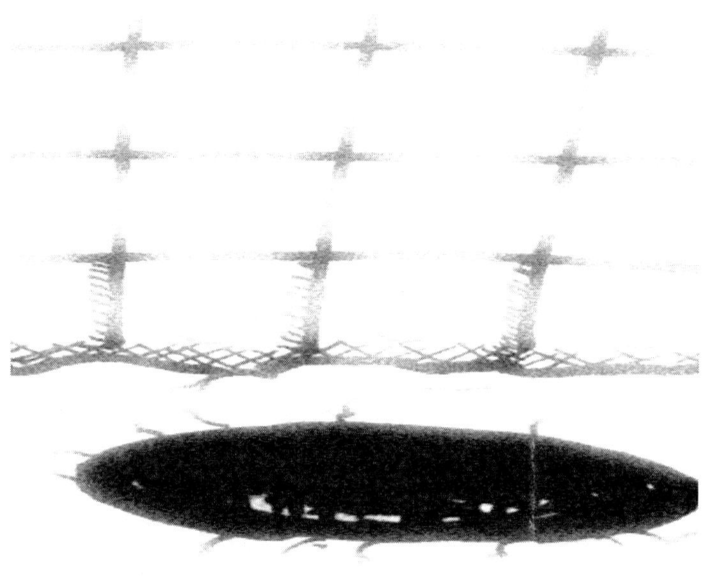

Compassion fiddled with the small recorder at a corner of the room "Alright Virtue, I've turned on your recorder. You may now slide down the tunnel. As always, have a safe trip. See you in exactly 26 hours."

Virtue pursed her lips and chucked her index and middle finger up as if to say *deuces*. Before I knew it, she hopped into the large open birthing tunnel.

"Dammit! I forgot to ask her how she chose to make her entrance." I snapped my fingers in regret.

"Mind if I take a quick look at her entrance?" I asked Passion timidly.

She sighed and looked up, waiting for an answer from Virtue's advisor, who was observing from another room.

A loud booming voice answered from the speakers. *"It's fine. But only because I know Virtue won't mind, otherwise this would break our confidentiality policy."*

I smiled in gratitude as I thanked Virtue's sensei. "Thank you, Honor."

Passion led me to one of the blinking green lights and tapped her index finger on the plastic-like protective covering of the light in a systematic rhythm. The flicker of light expanded into a viewing tube. "Make it quick, I have another participant coming in soon." She advised as she rushed off.

The screen was black and then slowly the blackness dissolved into a sea of bright blurry colors. I heard a loud SMACK and heard the piercing cry of a baby. A beige man in blue scrubs appeared as the frame came into focus. He had the bottom half of this face covered in surgical gear, leaving only his slanted eyes and shiny coal black hair exposed. His hair was slicked to the side with a part. I watched as he peered into the recorder, or rather the eyes of baby Virtue.

A woman, who I presumed was a nurse, appeared by the man's side. She had the same dramatically slanted eyes and pale skin. I quickly processed the translation as she told the man in Japanese, "She doesn't want to see the baby. She's giving the baby away." The man quickly nodded his head in acknowledgment, dismissing the nurse.

Baby Virtue was still crying. "*Now, now.*" The man cooed. "Your mother is only a child herself. I'm sure you'll find a nice family."

I was disappointed when Compassion made her way back and turned off the monitor. "Time to go, our subject arrived earlier than expected."

I hurried and departed from the room. With the exception of Virtue, I hated to witness arrivals. The confusion and fear was always hard to watch and I always found myself releasing a breath that I hadn't known I was holding in once their memories returned. It was always tough trying to explain to the participants that they were back in the realm of consciousness and that life and death did not exist without us. That we were all members of consciousness.

I made my way to the librarium and thought about looking for an empty spot on the floor. If I did that, it would signify to the other members that I was on the market for constructing a new mortal family and whoever wished to be a member my family had to sit beside me and call dibs on their role in the family; whether it were as a mother, brother, father or sister. Once a 4-member family unit was complete, the designated mother and father would have to travel through the birthing tunnel first and then their designated offspring would slide down after some time had passed. If I chose not to form and construct a new family than I would be randomly assigned to a family once I traveled through the birth canal.

For the time being, I grabbed a Life Plan form from the librarium and slipped into one of the empty classrooms to prepare for my next life.

LIFE PLAN

ID#: 9999.99999 **RANK:** *Patience*

ADVISOR: Sensei Respect

LIFETIME LEVEL: *(please note, if "Difficult" is chosen, the possibility of suicide is highly likely)*: Difficult

TIME PERIOD: *Early 1800s*

LIFE ASPIRATIONS:

Abolitionist to help lead the enslaved to freedom using a secret system of safe houses, similar to an underground railroad type network.

LIFE GENDER (MALE/FEMALE/RANDOM DRAW): Random draw

EXIT PLAN: Pneumonia

EXIT AGE: *Age 90*

PILFERED RECOLLECTIONS

A flash fiction

Someone had spanked me too hard on my ass. It hurt like hell and I had remembered from the other dimension that that would happen. I just hadn't expected it to hurt that much.

I was spanked again.

I could hear my spirit guide's voice reminding me, "*If you do not cry, they will continue to spank, therefore you must cry out at once.*"

I cried out in genuine exasperation.

I was carried to another room and cleaned up. I was then taken to another room where other new participants were laying inside small containers. They were all bundled up in thin pink and blue blankets and had on white beanie-looking caps on their heads. I recognized a few of them from back home.

Faith, is that you? I asked telepathically when the person carrying me stopped to lay me down in one of those clear containers. I had turned my head and recognized Faith laying in the container beside me.

Faith looked over at me. *Yeah it's me. I just got here not too long ago. I think I hear someone coming. I wonder who else is here. Did we all really choose the same day to make our entrance?*

I laughed, happy to bump into someone I knew.

I heard the sounds of tapping heels. The sound stopped near me and a face of a wombman peered in my container. The wombman lifted me slowly from out the box.

It was *Serenity*! I wanted to laugh at the unexpected reunion.

Her eyes were wet as she made eye contact with me. Although she looked very different in this reality, I could still see and recognize her blue aura perfectly. Apparently, we had both come back as beings of Asian descent. I wondered what country I had born in this time. More importantly, I wonder if she remembered me.

Serenity! It me, Virtue! I thought to myself, knowing damn well that telepathy did not exist in this dimension. Well it *did*, but we were all well aware back at our real home that our pineal abilities in this dimension were stagnant due to the food, music and other factors that impaired the pineal gland. It was such a shame, too.

Serenity kissed me delicately on the forehead. "I'm going to take very good care of you. I'll be the best mother to you, I promise."

A man that I had seen around the librarium back at home, but never was never really acquainted with appeared by Serenity's side and gave her a kiss on the cheek before giving me one on the forehead. "We finally have our baby girl. I told you honey. I knew she wouldn't change her mind about giving up the baby."

What were they talking about?

Serenity sniffled, "I can't believe we finally have our own baby. But what if she changes her mind later and decides she wants to keep her baby? I'm almost scared to get too happy. This seems like a dream."

That's because this realm isn't even real, it's a learning environment. I laughed inside.

"Look honey, did you see that? She just smiled!" Serenity announced excitedly. *Crap*, I hadn't meant to do that but I felt really happy to be able to bring a smile to her face, she was such a beautiful and compassionate soul back home.

A nurse entered the room. "Mrs. Ying, we need to give the baby some shots."

Oh no, the dreaded shots.

I was passed to the nurse who took me to another room and placed me gently in another container. She held a syringe filled with clear liquid and then used her middle finger and thumb to flick at it. She held it up to the light and then stared at the liquid as she gave it another flick. Seemingly satisfied, she made her way towards me.

Noooo, please don't. I wailed in displeasure.

"Shhh, this will only be a second." The nurse assured me.

I continued to wail. I knew there was nothing I could do. I was too small to fight back. I knew, as we all knew back home, that once I was injected with this poison, my telepathy and other "super-natural" abilities would lay dormant. I knew that my recollection and knowledge of back home would be immediately forgotten until I returned home.

I kicked and gave one last wail as I experienced the violation of the pilferage of my powers and memories.

CHANGES

A flash fiction

Inspired by the song Changes by the late Tupac Amaru Shakur

"Man, I can't believe they still haven't figured this shit out yet." Sirius scratched his head, gazing down at the marble-like sphere called Earth, in disappointment.

Venus, who was sitting across from Sirius, and staring just as intently at the globe snickered. "'Don't forget that we were just as clueless when we were living down there."

Orion, who was also sitting and watching the activity added, "Oh trust me, I remember and I definitely don't miss it down there. Too much chaos, sadness and low vibrational activity."

Sirius smiled as he reminisced. "Well, I had a blast while I was there."

Venus tilted her head to the side at Sirius. "We couldn't all get to be a rap superstar like you. I actually wasted my entire time being a racist bigot. If I had only known what I know now." She shook her head in regret as she thought of the time she had wasted.

Orion nodded in agreement. "I know what you mean. I wasn't racist but I allowed myself to get sucked in by the media, believing every lie from the television. You think they'll ever figure out the remedy to all this chaos? I mean it's so simple."

"Who knows." Venus answered, "Some will eventually wake up and get it and others will laugh at the enlightened few."

Sirius disagreed. "Nah, I think they'll eventually figure it out. It'll take some time but they'll eventually get it. I have faith in humanity. Not to mention, the veils separating the dimensions are thinning. We just have to make sure we're there to assist them when the time is right."

"Ya'll still checking on 'em? You'd think you guys were watching a football game the way you keep up with them." Aries teased as she joined the trio, placing herself between Venus and Sirius.

Sirius chuckled. "Might as well be. See that guy over there" He pointed. "That guy is Dermin McDaniel. He's running for president and that woman right there is Sage Hilaire. He's running against her."

Aries shrugged playfully at Sirius. "So? This isn't the first one we've ever seen."

"True but check this: Dermin and Hilaire are actually playin' everybody."

"Whatchu mean?" Aries interrupted, intrigued.

"Hold on, I'm getting to that." He laughed. "See, doesn't matter who gets elected, everyone still end up getting played by the puppeteer."

Aries raised a brow. "Interesting. And no one knows this?"

Venus answered. "There are a few who have figured it out. Unfortunately, a lot of people that I used to be associated with are falling for the gimmicks." She shook her head. "McDaniel is pitting black against white and poor against the wealthy and all that's doing is adding to the chaos."

"What chaos?" Aries asked, trying her best to catch up on the drama transpiring on Earth.

Sirius chuckled at her unawareness. "Police brutality and systemic racism and prejudices against not only blacks but also Muslims and Mexicans. I rapped a lot about it while I was there. I also talked a lot about unity among the oppressed."

Orion nodded. "I remember and it's a shame that it made little impact especially seeing that you're still held in high regard. Which is why I doubt they'll ever get it."

"Get what?" Aries asked as she stared curiously at the globe.

Sirius answered. "That the *only* way to change the world is through unity among all mankind."

Aries snickered in skepticism.

Sirius nodded as he turned towards her. "Think about it. As we all now recognize, there is no such thing as race. There is only one race. The *human* race. The term was only invented to support slavery. Those who can understand this concept are the truly enlightened."

"Smoke and mirrors." Orion chimed.

"Mass deception, mass control...." Venus included.

"Carolus Linneaus and Johann Blumenbach. Remember them?" Sirius asked.

With the exception of Aries, they all nodded.

"Race is all just a man-made concept." Sirius informed solemnly. "The way I see it, if they keep letting the media, including social media control their emotions,-"

Aries interrupted. "If *who* continue to let the media control their emotions?"

"*Everyone*. Blacks and whites. Rich and Poor. Celebrities and non-celebrities. If they keep letting the puppeteers continue to deceive them, the cycle will just continue. White against black because of the media and black against white as a result. There is even a new rising of blacks who deem themselves superior than whites."

"Just like how the whites started out. And the cycle continues." Venus shook her head.

"Ohhh." Aries nodded.

"And guess who's sitting back laughing?" Sirius asked, "The evil ones. But in the meantime, blacks need to come together in unity and uplift one another and stop killing themselves with the way they eat. As well as support one another in business ventures and love themselves and each other."

Aries put her index finger to her chin as she thought. "So let me get this straight. Your solution is loving each other? Black and whites?"

"You're finally getting' it. We're all connected. We're all *one*. The answer is loving one another. Think about *all* of the great respected legends who have been a big influence in society and would not have been in existence had their parents not procreated with a different so-called '*race*'. We got Farrakhan, Barack Obama-"

"Bob Marley." Orion interjected.

"Malcolm X and some might even say J. Cole." Venus added with a chuckle.

"So you're saying that they should love their enemies?" Aries asked with a raised brow, held up by doubt.

"Nope!" Sirius grinned half-heartedly. "I believe in an eye for an eye. What I'm saying is *everyone* needs to become the change they wanna see; especially for these future generations. They must be willing to dig deeper and find the truth. To elevate their frequency. Love is at a much higher frequency than hate and fear. They gotta stop letting these puppeteers control who they hate, who they love, and who to pray for. We're all just energy and we don't always come back as the same skin color each lifetime."

"Aahh, I see." Aries nodded slowly.

Sirius, Venus, Orion and Aries stared intently at the sphere-shaped globe, called Earth, in wonder.

"We gotta make a change.

It's time for us as a people to start makin' some changes.

Let's change the way we eat, let's change the way we live,

and let's change the way we treat each other.

You see the old way wasn't working. So it's on us to do

what we gotta do...to survive."- Tupac Shakur (Changes)

SLEEPING GIANTS
(PART 2)

A flash fiction

"Davis, wake up, we have a problem."

The young reptilian elite prodded Davis, the older reptilian, snoring besides him. The younger reptilian's green eyes were widened in fear the entire time. They were both seated inside of the highly secured Central Intelligence Control Room in front of a dozen or so small monitors, switches and buttons. It was only the elites and their families who had regular access to the dome-shaped underground facility.

Davis stirred and mumbled unintelligibly as the younger reptile continued with his rapid jabs. A river of drool slithered its way down Davis' bumpy emerald arm, onto a growing pool of saliva assembling right between the two creatures, on top of the metal desk.

"Biscuits? No biscuits today, mum." Davis smacked his lips before continuing to mumble in his sleeping state.

The younger reptilian gave Davis a sharp elbow to the ribs. "Wake up, you fool!" He bellowed irritably.

"I called Bingo!" Davis jumped up clumsily in a state of disarray, his arms flailing in every direction, causing an empty tea mug to come to a crash between them.

"You incompetent idiot! Have someone summon my father on the video monitor at once! Tell him, that *THEY* have awakened!" He exclaimed impatiently, a hint of fear exposed between his commands.

"Who? Who has awakened, sire?" Davis queried.

The younger reptilian flapped both arms as he tried explaining in alarm. "The sleeping giants! The Negus! The paradigm shift! One by one they're all awakening!"

"The Negus? But—but—they should still be combating against one another about frivolous so-and-so's, race, religion, orientation and other so-and-and so's? Right, Argon? Argon?" The older reptilian quizzed as he stood eye to eye from Argon, the smell of mice and American blueberry biscuits permeating the close quarters between them. Their noses touched as Davis anticipated an answer. Argon remained silent as his body began to tremor.

"Argon?"

Instead of Argon's usual hurling of obscenities and impatience towards the older creature, the younger reptilian crumpled to the ground like limp noodles, not caring two bits that he had landed right on top of the sharp shattered mug. He could not feel an ounce of the physical pain anyway.

Argon, tilted his scaly chin towards the ceiling as he cried, "We're through! We're through! It's all over! They've awakened! We're all bloody throooough!"

MAMA AFRICA

by Rich H.

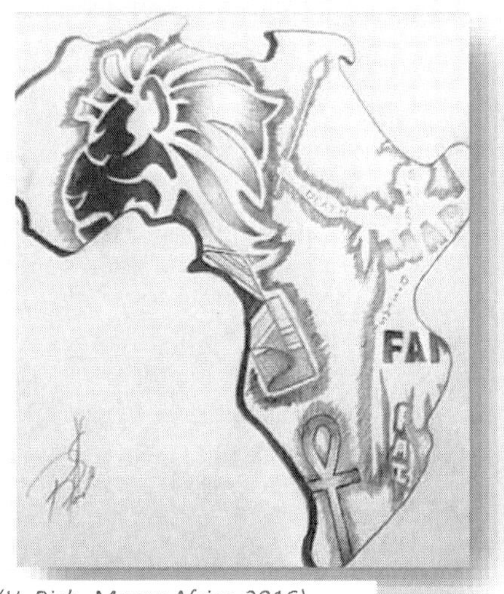

(H, Rich. Mama Africa.2016)

You have nurtured
my spirit and wa-
tered my soul...

From the trees,
rivers, and valleys

I can hear your
cries...

The days of enjoy-
ing life with the
abundance of
tribes are now
scarce...

Women and children starving...

Left to the decomposition of husband's and father's bullet
riddled bodies...
Who will protect you from the hardships of war famine and
drought....

From the Earth air water and flame I can hear your cries...

Children lay scattered across the streets lost and driven from their homes....

Thoughts of better days washed away with the blood of the innocent...

Shall we rise up and seek peace...

Shall we stand firm in our demand for equality...

Shall we fight back as true warriors....

Protecting the rights liberties and freedoms of our melanated brothas and sistas...

Through the splash of the flowing rivers, the whistles of the lively trees, and by the echoes of the valley's crest

Mama Africa I can hear your cries...

THE MELANINS

Beings from another dimension have landed on Earth to conduct research on the inhabitants of Earth. They are disturbed by the treatment of each other, the amount of work for the majority of a human's lifetime, as well as the mind control that the majority seem to be oblivious of. The most unsettling of all is the discovery of a royal species on Earth. They are in fact the most despised group of the planet. The operators of mind control are the only ones who know truth and use every attempt of mass deception and control to bury the truth to accumulate and hold on to wealth and power. This seems almost blasphemous to the visitors of Earth as the Melanins are the true rulers and royal people back at their homeland. They ultimately discover that they were really sent to Earth on a mission to help release the royals from psychological enslavement.

Chapter One

Dear 1111,

We have arrived to our destination with no harm. The screen that the elders applied to us works excellently. At first we were a bit apprehensive to walk among them for fear of detection but the Earthlings are none the wiser. We cannot be felt or seen and we are able to walk through matter. I am assuming this is what the visitation experience is like for the Wisers when they pass on to their next lifetime.

I must also say that the Earthlings seem to always be in motion or preoccupied. There seems to always be work to be done. Someone is always managing or occupying an establishment that I've learned is referred to as a "business", which fits perfectly as they always seem to be "busy". However not all of these beings work or run an establishment. We stumbled upon a building where the miniature Earthlings are divided by height, I assume, and sit in a room while a normal sized Earthling stand at the front of the room.

There is also another facility that we discovered. The atmosphere seemed harsher and there were full sized Earthling there, all the same gender. The schedule and activities there were a bit similar to the activities at the facility for the miniature Earthlings except that the full sized Earthlings slept at the other facility and never left. Both had a time to consume energy, both had to ask permission to do certain things and both had an increment of play time outdoors. There were also attacks in each facility however, strangely enough, the attacks came from their own...from each other on one another. A strange and disturbing thing to witness indeed. The more violent attacks were at the facility where the full sized Earthlings were kept. Day one has truly been full of intrigues. Send my regards to 96513 and the royal court. 7786 also sends regards.

Chapter Two

Day two

1111,

Excuse our tardiness in our response. We received your communication but the most peculiar thing happened. The firmament altered and due to the sun disappearing the telepen would not function until the sun appeared again. Another strange thing happened when the sun disappeared. The busyness of the beings slowed down. It did not however come to a complete halt. 7786 and I need to consume some energy so we will give you an update after we have refilled. I will be sure to send photographs as requested

Chapter Three

1111,

7786 and I agreed to separate, observe, and later compare records.

Although we were assured by our fellow technologists back home that we had absolutely nothing to fret about, out of precaution we have decided that the only safe place to keep our transporter is underneath the Pacific Ocean. We aren't sure how advanced these beings are in their technology as of yet. So until we are certain we must take all precautions on this mission.

Chapter Four

Day five

1111,

The heavens have shifted in hue five times since we have landed here. Our conclusion is that the sun disappears and returns recurrently at the same exact interval. All activity seems to revolve around the disappearance and reappearance of the sun.

Have the technologists yet figured out what the rectangular objects are in the photograph?

7786 and I have come up with several theories:

- Advanced equipment used to lower the frequency of energy refill.

- Telecommunication device to communicate with their queen.
- A device that instructs them on their obligations or duties in increments as the device seems to be used periodically during business time and habitually after.

We are working on finding a way to have one of these devices in our possession. That feat in itself has proved to be quite the task as these devices seem to always be in the clutches of these beings. Perhaps it is of some sort of lifeline? We are eager to learn from our expert technologists on what purpose these devices serve these beings.

The device is always a short distance away. It must be a lifeline as we have both seen the beings in panic when the device is missing. This reason alone makes it a difficult task in obtaining the device for research. Perhaps a disguise would be suitable to assist us in this assignment? Beige in color, for that is the color of these creatures.

Chapter Five

1111,

7786 and I were successful in securing the device and it was all thanks to the disguises sent. Although the feat was still a great one, we give our absolute gratitude!

Upon examination of the device, we discovered that the device is an old rendition of our Zykis. The creatures here are not as advanced as originally presumed. These devices can only make calls, send and receive data, and take photographs for the most part. Unlike our Zykis, which is 5,000 light years ahead.

Also, we received your message about the Melanins. We have not seen any. Perhaps there is another planet that they can be found? 7786 is still under the adamant that the tale of the

Melanins is just that: a myth. I must admit, 7786 almost convinced me that it has to be a myth. For how could we have lost connection with our royals? Surely there would have been a log of which planet the Melanins had landed on to assist in the advancement of civilization. It just does not make sense. Especially after so much time have passed. Millenniums!

****

Dear 1111,

7786 ask that you please send our regards to our loved ones.

Please send our deepest apologizes to the royal court. We had not meant to infuriate or anger the royal ones with our last communication. We will do all that we can to find the noble Melanins. We will travel to each corner of this planet to locate them and fulfill our duty. We had not known that this was what we had been sent to do. This is such a great and intimidating task to fulfil that one can understand why we were not told our task until we arrived.

I do have great news! We were able to finally test out our translators and they work impeccably. However, that isn't the great news. We met a very nice female being and were able to learn that we are in a place of the planet called Beijing, China. This is why we had not seen any Melanins. We were able to speak to a resident in their native language. Apparently, the Melanins are scattered throughout this planet. When 7786 asked where we could find them, the female being gave us confused looks but laughed and mentioned a place called Africa. Is it possible for the technologists to assist us in locating "Africa"? Perhaps this was not a myth after all. 7786 is still in doubt. As you know 7786 is a very knowledgeable student in the history of the royal bloodline of the Melanins. Of course, now that I think of it, that I'm sure was the reason he was chosen to join me on this trek.

As I was saying, 7786 is in doubt. 7786 is adamant that the Melanins had landed in a place called Alkebulan, not Africa. Nevertheless, we shall continue on to Africa.

Please send my regards to 96513.

Chapter Six

Day sixteen

1111,

7786 and I apologize for the extended delay. We were terribly ill from consuming the energy that the beings call "food" on this planet. The energy is an acquired taste. I don't think the energy is as good for the being's body as they have been led to believe. We saved some of the "food" and later used our scanner on the transporter to examine and test the energy. The one called *fish* was filled with harmful mercury and other toxins. We were also horrified to learn that we were indeed eating what we call back home *Hakquans*! I do believe that is what caused our ill fate, as we know that our species do not believe in the consumption and suffering of other living beings. We also believe that the “food” here has been tinkered with and modified. The beings here do have other type of energy that they call *processed food*. After sampling and testing, our tests revealed that there are a number of different chemicals injected and used.

There was one sandy textured ingredient in many of the food that we learned was called refined *sugar*. It is the most detrimental of all so far. We believe this is the main aggressor and contributor to the progressive aging and cell damage. The beings do not seem to be aware of this, as they feed their offspring this poison. It must also be noted that almost *every* single “food” here has this poison.

However, the chemicals have a very delightful taste! We have found in an unfortunate way, that some components of the additives are for addictive purposes. You see, after having sampled a few processed foods under the category of what they refer to as “sweets”, we began to experience a deep yearning for more. We have finally weaned off of the poison for good after numerous fails, with no intentions of ever consuming it again.

7786 and I are worried that perhaps the Melanins have used their power to corrupt the planet with mass deception?

Speaking of deception, we decided to throw out the device we had procured. We discovered from the female being that it is called a “cellular phone”. We tested the device as well and we were horrified to learn the amount of radiation emitted from the device. We also found out that the lifespan of these beings are only up to one century! After learning about their tampered energy source, food, and their numerous amount of radiological emitted devices, it is surely no surprise that our lifespan is 20 times longer!

Perhaps all that we had learned about the Melanins back home were not total truth? Perhaps they had been sent to this planet due to their evil nature? Surely they cannot be as kind and generous as the majestic Melanins back home. Why would they be determined to harm their subjects in this way?

7786 and I are disappointed in our discoveries so far. Please do not relay our revelations of the royal Melanins on this planet until we have finished our exploration, as we do not want to anger the royal court again. We are heading to Africa as soon as the heavens shift in hue again.

Chapter Seven

1111,

7786 and I have some great news and also a bit of disturbing news as well.

Let's start with the good news. We have arrived in Africa! We discovered we had landed at a village called Kangbe located in a place named, Sierra Leone. This is where we found the Melanins!

The other good news is that they are not the wicked rulers that 7786 and I were starting to believe they were. They are actually just as kind, generous and intelligent as the royals back home. They are just as beautiful in hue.

The unfortunate news is very troubling, the Melanins are not the rulers of this planet as we had left them. They have somehow been thrown off of the throne. The alarming part is that the royals are very oppressed and living in appalling conditions! The most upsetting and worrying part of it all is that the Melanins have no clue that they are sovereign and part of a royal blood line! They do not know they are royalty! When 7786 and I saw the first Melanin, a female, we respectably bowed with our face to the ground, as is the custom back home. She backed away and the other Melanins in the distant began to laugh at us. Imagine our surprise.

We made friends with an elderly male Melanin. I suspect that he knew that we were not from this planet. He often brought up the Dogon Tribe and asked if we were here to visit them. We told him that we were in search of the mysterious place of Alkebulan but had been unsuccessful. That is when he informed 7786 and I that *Alkebulan was Africa!* He asked if we could take him back home with us although we had never given him any inclination that we were from a different planet. We had worn our disguises so we are still not sure how he knew. Perhaps what we had learned back home about the Melanins here are true in regards to their majestic third eye?

The elderly Melanin allowed us to stay with him for 3 days. He taught a lot about the history and plight of the royal Melanins since the time of their arrival here. 7786 and I wept. For the information is indeed very disheartening, tragic and traumatic; so much so that I wish not to repeat it.

7786 and I both agree that the royal courts must be notified of this at once and help must be sent for rescue and to help conquer back the throne!

The elderly Melanin suggested we visit another location on this planet where there are many Melanins. A small place called

America. He stated that It was not as big as Africa nor did it contain as many natural resources but he was very insistent. So the land of America shall be our next stop.

To be continued in Negus vol. 2........

If you enjoyed NEGUS, please check out an excerpt from

Black Out

What happens when residents of St. Molasses, MS, a town high with racial tension, start waking up one by one in the color they despise?

Black Out

PROLOGUE

It all began like the arrival of a California earthquake on a still autumn morning. No signs, no warnings, not even an omen. One minute thirteen-year-old Rusty Haynes Jr. was fast asleep in his parent's two-bedroom trailer, and the next minute, his ma was standing over him with a tattered straw broomstick. If that weren't strange enough, he was stunned to find his pa aiming a 1957 Remington rifle right at him. Both were still in their pajamas.

"What the hell are you doing in my boy's bed?" Rusty Sr. shouted.

Rusty Jr. crinkled his brows. "*Hunh?*"

Judy Haynes began swatting at the boy's head. "Where is he, *nigger?!*"

Rusty Jr.'s heart sped as he tried to block his mother's attacks. "What's goin' on?"

"I'll handle this." Rusty Sr. said to his wife.

He slowly took a step forward until the barrel of the Remington was pressed firmly against the boy's forehead. The sinister look in his blue eyes frightened his son.

"Listen here, nigger, you got 'xactly three seconds to tell me what you've done with Rusty, or I'm fixin' to put a hole right through that thick nigger skull of yours."

The boy's heart palpitated as he pleaded, "Pa! *It's me!*"

"What you call me?"

Rusty Sr. swung the butt of the rifle at the boy's head but wasn't fast enough. The boy grabbed the long barrel and pushed it against his father's stomach as they both began tussling for control of the gun.

"Pa! It's me!" The boy shouted, with tears clouding his eyes.

"Judy!" Rusty Sr. hollered. "Help me out here!"

Judy stood frozen behind them with both her hands covering her mouth. They were both moving about so quickly, she didn't know what to do.

She finally dashed out the bedroom, ran through their quaint living room, and into the kitchen to grab a large butcher knife. Just as she was making her way back to her son's bedroom, she heard a deafening blast throughout the small trailer.

"Russell?! Russ!!" Judy hollered.

Her flimsy blue house slippers ran to the bedroom and halted at the gruesome sight of her husband lying on the dull hardwood floor, with a pool of blood rushing from the side of his head.

The blood continued to spill out of the hole in his cranium, as she held his head onto her lap. *"Rusty! Rustyyyyy!"*

"Mama, I didn't mean to! Honest, I didn't!" Rusty Jr. sobbed. His hands trembled as he held on to the rifle.

Enraged, Judy Haynes grabbed the butcher knife from beside her and swiftly leapt to her feet to charge at the colored boy.

"*Mama! No!*" He cried out. Desperate, he aimed the rifle directly at the woman.

Unaffected by the threat of the gun, Judy Haynes attempted to plunge the butcher knife into his chest but missed. She continued to flail the butcher knife wildly, while threatening to chop his limbs to pieces. Rusty tripped onto the ground, causing the gun to slip from his hand. He recoiled and braced himself for the brutal pain that he knew was sure to come with being butchered alive. That is, until he spotted the rifle at his side.

CHAPTER ONE

Russell Haynes Jr. was born thirteen years ago to Russell Haynes Sr. and Judith Michelle Haynes. Mr. and Mrs. Haynes had three children altogether: Nathaniel, Julia, and Rusty Jr.. Their oldest, Nathaniel Haynes, had been killed years ago during combat in Vietnam at the age of twenty. Their only daughter, Julia Haynes, had run away to San Francisco right after high school with Seymour Montgomery, a colored boy. Both Rusty Sr. and Judy Haynes disowned their daughter after discovering she had married Seymour and given birth to their only granddaughter, Jordyn Rose Montgomery, whom they also disowned. News travelled fast in Saint Molasses, and for years the Haynes would become the topic of all gossip amongst men and women, coloreds and whites alike. Negroes and whites running off together was not only unheard of, but frowned upon in Saint Molasses.

The small Mississippi town of Saint Molasses had a population of barely 800. In fact, the town was so small, there was only one library, one school, one pharmacy, and one major grocery store. If one wished to visit a museum, shopping mall, night club, or movie theater, they'd have to travel a couple miles over to the city of Marmalade to do so.

Like most small rural towns, everybody knew everybody. Depending on what you were up to, that could either be a good thing or a bad thing. For instance, if you had a passion for chasing skirts, like Sonny O'Donnell, then it was probably a bad thing. Just ask Mrs. O'Donnell, who demanded her husband take his "whores" to the inn over in Marmalade if he insisted on cheating. She'd grown tired of being a recurring topic of the town's gossip. That's the type of thing that came with being a resident of a small town. Everyone knew everyone. Which would explain why Frederick, a visitor, had been receiving odd looks ever since his Plymouth Fury had overheated, right in front of the town's welcome sign.

It had taken almost an entire day for nineteen-year-old Frederick King to find an auto shop that would fix his automobile. Every mechanic he'd brought his vehicle to had either outright told him they didn't service coloreds or had given him a quote of an astronomical figure. He finally ran into a townsman at a local drug store who was willing to point him in the right direction, but by that time, night was slowly creeping in.

"There's a mechanic shop, Lucky Man's Auto & Repair." The white gentleman said, whose hair reminded Frederick of Elvis Presley. He pointed east, then said, "Just head down that road and make the first left. Can't miss it."

"Thanks a lot, sir." Frederick said. Heading towards his car, he heard the man mumble something. "You say somethin'?"

"I said," The man began, drawing near. "I said, it's almost seven. Everything's fixin' to close in a few minutes."

"Y'all got any motels around here?"

"Next town over." The man answered.

"How far is that?"

"'Bout a few miles."

Frederick glanced back at his Plymouth. "Think she'll make it?"

The man looked at the ten-year-old car. "Can't say. Where ya' from?" The man asked, curiously eyeing the younger man's Timberland boots, baggy jeans, and black fitted cap with a giant white X printed across it.

"Negus."

"Negus." The man repeated. "I reckon it's been a helluva lot of years since I been outta Saint Molasses. Don't think I can say I ever heard of it."

"You wouldn't have heard of it." Freddie informed.

The man furrowed his brows. "I don't catch ya' drift."

"Thanks for ya help, sir." He said, ignoring the confusion on the man's face. "You were the only person willing to help a brother out. Appreciate that."

The man's cheek's flushed with embarrassment. "I wouldn't call it helping."

"*Hey*." Margaret Browne, one of the oldest residents in town, called out. A round white woman with sky blue hair, the widow was known as the town's busiest busybody. She squinted in their direction before asking, "Everything alright?"

The white man lifted a hand. "Everything's alright, Mrs. Browne."

"I don't mind going back in to have Albert phone the sheriff." She offered, pointing at the drug store.

"It's alright, Mrs. Browne." He repeated more firmly. He turned his attention back to the young man. "You'd best hurry along and go on to the next town if I were you. Quickly."

Freddie nodded. "You're not from around here yourself, are you?" Freddie asked.

The man peered into Freddie's eyes suspiciously. He blinked when he thought he'd seen the iris of the boy's eyes flicker blue. "Originally from Dayton. Dayton, Ohio. Is it that obvious?" He smiled.

Freddie pressed his lips together as he smiled back. "Thanks for your generosity, sir. I gotta get going." He said. He was about to turn towards his vehicle when he halted, as if suddenly remembering something. "Don't you forget where you came from, Jimmy. Don't ever forget."

Before he could ask how he'd known his name, the young man, and his Plymouth Fury vanished into thin air.

Bug-eyed, Jimmy turned to face Margaret. "Did ya' see-" His voice trailed off as he watched the elderly woman's body go limp. With her dark brown eyes still stretched open in shock, he rushed to her side before her body could hit the concrete.

CHAPTER TWO

"Police are asking anyone who may have any information on the brutal slaying of Russell Haynes Senior and Judith Haynes, as well as the disappearance of their thirteen-year-old son, Russell Haynes Jr., to please contact the sheriff's office at...." The news anchor spouted off the number as a photo of a smiling Rusty Jr. with bright red hair was shown on screen.

"Isn't it just horrible?" Georgia Daniels asked, cupping a slender hand over her red painted lips. "We shouldn't have to hear about this on the day of Judy Garland's death. I'm depressed enough as it is."

Jimmy squinted at the black-and-white television in their living room. "Russell and Judith Haynes? Isn't that-"

Georgia's full blonde ringlets bounced as she interrupted, "Don't you remember? Mr. Haynes is the short fella with the red hair who works at that janky ol' car lot."

Jimmy eyes lit up in recognition as he nodded. "That's right. He tried to sell us that yellow Mustang for three times the price, when I specifically asked for the Thunderbird. Eyes lit up soon as you told him I was a lawyer. Con artist is what he is."

Georgia's eyes filled with fear as she shoved her husband. "The man is dead, Jimmy! And the killer is still out there somewhere."

"I'm sure they'll catch the bastard sooner than later. There's only so many places you can hide in this town."

Georgia scooted closer to him as she whispered, "They even killed his poor wife! It could've easily been me. I'm home alone all day while you're at work. The maid is only here for a coupla' hours every morning."

"Maybe you can hang out over at Eugenia's while I'm at work until the killer is caught. Hell, you could always pick up a part-time job so you're not at home alone during the day."

"A *job*? This isn't a joke, Jimmy." Georgia replied. "May the good Lord find Rusty Jr. Poor kid. Shoot, maybe I will drive over to Eugenia's during the day. Eugenia and Oliver just bought a nice big RCA color television set. It'd be downright groovy to watch Guiding Light in color."

Jimmy groaned, knowing that it was only a matter of time before Georgia would start pestering him to buy a color T.V.

"Told you we should've moved to Ohio." Georgia said.

Jimmy frowned. "You don't know anyone in Ohio. Why on earth would we move out there?"

"That's beside the point." She said. "You have family in Dayton. It's not like we would've been totally alone."

He shifted uneasily. "I told you, I haven't spoken to them in years. Besides, I'm sure you and Eugenia would miss each other if we moved."

Georgia held onto his arm. "You might have a point. Eugenia's like a sister to me." She sighed. "I don't know why they just don't run those people out of town." Georgia pouted.

"What people?"

Georgia scowled. "Those nig—those coloreds." She quickly corrected herself, remembering the fight she and her husband had gotten into the last time she had called their maid a nigger.

He gave her a quizzical look. "What have they ever done to you?" He asked. "Our housekeeper's colored for god sake."

She reared her head back as her blue eyes widened. "Who cares? They're *all* savages. Police said the killer was a darkie. We've done nothing but helped these people by providing them with jobs and education and whatnot, and this is how they repay us?"

Jimmy shook his head in disagreement. "They also said they had never seen a colored man with blue eyes in Saint Molasses before. It was confirmed that the killer was an outsider. It isn't any of the colored folks already living here, Georgia."

"They're all the same far as I'm concerned. They've all got the same jungle blood runnin' in 'em. This is the exact reason why I'm against integration." She spewed, crossing her arms. "Those animals just can't be tamed."

Jimmy shook his head in disdain.

"Only an animal would murder a helpless woman and child in cold blood, Jimmy."

"They didn't say the boy was murdered."

"Don't be so naïve. The boy is dead."

Jimmy pulled away from his wife and stood up from the sofa.

She looked up at him, suddenly afraid to be left alone. "Where yer goin'?"

Away from you, he wanted to say. "Jesus, can't a man take a leak without his wife givin' em the third degree?"

He walked off towards the bathroom, not waiting for a response from Georgia. Once inside, he immediately turned on the faucet and splashed the cold water on his face.

He stared at his reflection in the mirror. "Nah, it couldn't have been." He muttered to himself. "The boy they're lookin' for has blue eyes. He didn't have blue eyes. I'm almost sure of it." He didn't sound convincing even to himself. Had he imagined seeing the boy's eyes flicker blue? What if it was him? His wife was right. That could have easily been Georgia and himself murdered. He had almost invited the stranger to spend the night at their home, right before he just up and disappeared. Had he actually disappeared into thin air?

Don't you forget where you came from, Jimmy. Don't ever forget. What exactly had he meant by that?

CHAPTER THREE

Dressed in blue blood-stained flannel pajamas, Rusty sneakers slammed against the pavement as he literally ran for his life. Hearing sirens in the distance, he had no doubt they were en route to his parents' trailer.

It all felt like a dream to Rusty, like an alternate reality. One minute his parents were...well, his parents. The next, they were trying to kill him as if they hadn't raised him the last thirteen and a half years.

Sniffling, he used a sleeve to wipe his wet blue eyes. Slowing down to catch his breath, he spotted his junior high school's vacant baseball field. He ran towards the stadium, figuring he could hide beneath the bleachers.

Fitting snugly underneath the seats, Rusty released a soft sputter that sounded like a cough. He squeezed his eyes shut and held his mouth open as he sobbed quietly. He couldn't wrap his head around the fact that he was now an orphan or the fact that it had been *him* who had murdered his parents. Other than hunting for racoons and rabbits with his pa, Rusty Jr. had never taken a life.

He looked down at the pigment of his hands. For the umpteenth time, he tried rubbing the top of his hand with the sleeve of his pajamas as hard as he could. Whatever this was on his skin, would not rub off.

"*Good grief.*" He mumbled tearfully. The paint, or whatever it was, seemed to have set in deep.

Growing angrier by the second, Rusty scratched at his head in frustration. He leapt a few inches off the ground, bumping his head on the steel directly above him, at the feel of the coarse texture of his hair.

"*What in tarnation?!*" He cried, pulling at the puffy hair on his head. Yanking out a strand of hair, his eyes bucked at the sight of the tightly coiled dark red strand, instead of his own stringy bright red hair.

"*Mama.*" He sobbed longingly. His tears seemed to be never-ending as they cascaded over his cheeks and onto his soiled pajamas.

"*Somebody out here?*"

Rusty stiffened at the deep baritone of a man's voice calling out from the outfield.

"Anybody out here?" A much friendlier voice echoed.

Rusty held his breath as two pairs of patent leather shoes trudged in the grass towards the bleachers. They stopped a few feet away from him.

"There's no one here." Deep voice said. "Told you to take Mrs. Abbott's word with a grain of salt."

The second man sighed. "Well she seemed pretty adamant that she seen a colored boy run this way."

"That old wench is pushing a 'hunnet, Bailey. Could've been staring at a smudge on her spectacles for all we know."

The second man was skeptical. "Gave a pretty accurate description, you ask me. Same description the neighbor 'cross the street from the Haynes gave."

"There ain't nobody here and frankly, I just wanna get home to Earline's meat loaf and sweet potato pie." Deep voice admitted impatiently.

The second man sighed. "Alright. I'll let the sheriff know."

Rusty waited until he could no longer hear or see the patent leather shoes of the two men, before he stopped holding his breath. Had it been any other day, he would have asked for help. He would've turned himself in and explained why he had done what he did. How it had been an act of self-defense. How it had all been a bizarre day. He would've told it all, from start to finish. However, as young as he was, even he knew it would be stupid to expect them to help him. Not in a colored body, anyway. If there was one thing Saint Molasses, Mississippi was known for, it was their hatred of outsiders and niggers.

CHAPTER FOUR

"Sure it was a Plymouth?" Detective Dylan Ford's baritone voice probed.

"Positive." Margaret Browne answered, rearranging the dollies on her armchair, before taking a seat across from the two detectives. "Would you boys care for somethin' to drink?"

"No, thank you, ma'am." Detective Ford declined.

She looked at the other detective.

"No, thank you." Detective Edward Bailey replied. He looked down at his pocket-size notepad before proceeding. " Do you remember the color of the automobile, Mrs. Browne?"

Margaret squinted up at the ceiling as she stroked her chin. "I reckon it might've been red or brown. Maybe blue?"

Detective Ford threw his partner an exasperated glance. He had tried to tell Bailey before arriving at the old woman's two-story home, that getting reliable information from elderly residents had proven to be a waste of time.

"I know it was dark in color. I'm certain of it."

"And you're sure it was a nigger with blue eyes behind the wheel?" Ford questioned impatiently.

"No." Margaret scolded the detective. "I never said I seen him behind the wheel. He was outside the automobile when I seen him. I remember thinking that he looked like such a stranger nigger, with his blue eyes and strange clothes and what-not."

"Strange clothes?" Detective Bailey repeated.

She nodded. "Yes. He weren't dressed like the other niggers that live over yonder on the southside. His pants were too big, so was his shirt. He wore a baseball cap turned the wrong way. Oh, and his shoes! They weren't Oxfords or- what's the other ones?"

"Keds?" Bailey asked.

"Keds. They weren't those. Very strange-looking, know what I mean? Very suspicious looking colored."

"Did he go in the Brooks Pharmacy at all, ma'am?' Ford asked.

She shook her head. "I don't think so. I only seen him outside for about a coupla' minutes 'fore his car just vanished into thin air." Margaret Browne, explained.

Bailey looked up from his notepad. "Vanished?"

"Yes, Ed. Vanished. I reckon it's the craziest thing I ever did see in my seventy-somethin' years of livin'. I'm telling you, this is a prophecy straight out of the book of Revelations." She looked at Detective Ford. "I haven't seen you and Moriah at service lately past coupla' Sundays. Everything alright at home, Dylan?"

Detective Ford sighed as he ignored the busybody's interrogation. "Mrs. Browne, I'm gonna leave my card with my direct number on it. Please don't hesitate to call if you remember something else about that night."

"I sure will." She replied, accepting the business card.

"You have a great one, Mrs. Browne." Bailey said, rising from the plastic-covered suede sofa.

"Oh wait, I just remembered somethin'." Margaret announced. "Someone else was out there when all this went down." She informed.

"Who's that?" Ford asked.

"Jimmy."

"Jimmy?" Bailey repeated, jotting the name.

Margaret nodded. "Yes. I forget his last name. Can't remember much these days."

Again, Detective Ford looked at Bailey. They had wasted enough time.

Bailey refused to meet Ford's gaze. "Jimmy Sterling? The hog farmer?" He asked the old woman.

"No. Not that Jimmy. You know, that sharp rich fella married to that gorgeous blonde? She looks just like one 'em movie stars and he looks just like Elvis Presley. Those two are another one I haven't seen at church in months."

Ford snapped his fingers as his eyes lit up. "You talkin' about Jimmy Daniels?"

"Jimmy Daniels. That's the name." She smiled. "It's a good thing he was there when he was. Almost cracked my skull wide open, had it not been for Jimmy."

"Can you tell us why you think we should speak to Jimmy Daniels?"

"Jimmy and the nigger were outside talking for some time before the nigger and his car just-*poof*-disappeared into thin air." She explained.

This time, Detective Bailey met his partner's doubtful gaze.

"The car did what-now?" Ford questioned.

Mrs. Browne nodded. "Might sound crazy, but it just up and vanished. Right 'fore my eyes."

CHAPTER FIVE

Rusty waited for nightfall before trekking through his small town. On foot, Saint Molasses seemed much bigger to him. It was the first time he was grateful for the lack of city lights in Saint Molasses. He managed to find a half-eaten bear claw in the alley of the only Dixie Cream Donuts in town. He could have never in a million years imagine he would ever be so thankful to find a Dixie Cream cup filled with half-melted ice inside the dumpster. He spent the remainder of his night scrounging dumpsters in alleyways for anything he could salvage for later to eat.

Realizing that the following day would be a school day, Rusty decided that it was best not to retreat back to his junior high's baseball field. He jogged from the Dixie Cream donut shop and made his way to the Woolworth across the street. He discovered a dark corner behind the store near a loading dock, where a pile of cardboard boxes had been discarded. Rusty rummaged through the boxes until he found an empty Maytag box that had been used to hold a washing machine. He crawled inside the large box and tried his best to close the flaps of the box. With his stomach growling, Rusty began shoving the rest of the half-eaten and stale donuts he had saved for later. After having eaten the treats, he cried himself to sleep.

"Told you there was someone in there." Seventeen-year-old Lizzie Johnston whispered to Boo Harper the following morning. They both peered inside the large cardboard box to find a colored boy fast asleep inside.

"Hey, darkie! Get up!" Boo Harper shouted. "You're not allowed back here!"

"Ten more minutes, ma, please?" Rusty replied groggily.

Lizzie gasped as she squinted at his pajamas. "Is that blood?" She asked, covering her mouth with trembling hands.The sudden high-pitch scream of the teenaged girl jolted the boy awake.

"Oh, quit that hollerin'!" Boo demanded, covering his ears.

Startled, Rusty drew further into the box as he stared at Boo and Lizzie in Woolworth uniforms. Any other time, Liz would've asked how his pa, ma, and his schooling were doing. He, in response, would've answered with his usual generic reply. Every time he seen her, he thought about how his ma had told their neighbor that you could always count on Lizzie's ma to bring in the worse meat pie at the annual Toby county fair. Even now, he thought of this.

When Boo had finally gotten Lizzie to quit squawking, she cautiously peered into the opening of the cardboard again and gawked at the colored boy's eyes, which were as deep blue as her own. "It's him! It's him, it's him, it's him!"

Rusty could hear the shrieks of the seventeen-year-old girl as she ran off into the distance. He waited until Boo Harper disappeared from his view, before he quickly crawling out the box. He tried sprinting in the opposite direction of the Woolworth but was tackled facedown to the ground by Boo.

"Where do you reckon you're going, spook?" Boo asked, pinning Rusty to the ground. "You're gonna pay for what you've done to the Haynes. Rusty Jr. was one of my best friends." He lied. Boo Harper had always been a bully to Rusty Jr.

"Boo, it's me." Rusty cried out.

Boo narrowed his eyes, then held onto the back of the boy's pajamas as he dragged him to his feet. "What'd you say?"

"I said it's *me*. Rusty."

"How'd you know my name? Were you out here plotting to kill me?!" Boo shouted, looking around the parking lot, suddenly paranoid.

"No!" Rusty assured earnestly. Before he could convince him, Boo kneed him in the stomach. Rusty dropped to his knees as he wrapped his arms around his abdomen. He groaned until he his face was met with the sole of Boo's Oxfords.

"Don't cry like a pussy now." Boo snarled, secretly excited to have been the one to capture the Haynes killer.

"Is it him?" Rusty heard the approaching voice of another teenaged boy. He recognized him as the oldest brother of one of his classmates. His name was Charles but everyone in town called him Seven on account of him being born with only seven fingers. He had all five fingers on his right hand, and only his middle and index finger on his left.

"It's the sonofabitch all right." Boo confirmed.

"Sheriff's on his way. Said to be careful. He's considered armed and very dangerous."

"Don't look very dangerous to me." Boo said, as they both looked down at the crying boy.

"We oughta kill this sonofabitch." Seven taunted.

Boo chuckled. "Might as well. 'Bout as worthless as tits on a bull, you ask me." He said, before hawking a wad of phlegm at the boy's face.

Seven laughed as Rusty wiped the mucus off of his tear-stained cheeks. Seven, like Boo, couldn't help feeling a rush of excitement at finding the Haynes killer. He knew he'd finally be on the seven o'clock news. He'd always wanted to be on television.

"Can you hold on to 'em while I hit the bushes?" Boo asked. "Been holding it in since I got to work."

Seven nodded, grabbing the boy's arm with his good hand. "Go 'head and drain yer lizard, Boo. I got 'em."

"You sure?" Boo asked tentatively.

"I got it. Go on." Seven reassured.

Boo finally released his grip on Rusty's flannel shirt. Rusty and Seven both watched as he jogged towards some nearby bushes.

"This is all one big mix up. Please let me go." Rusty immediately pleaded.

"Now why would I go and do something like that? The Haynes trailer was right across from ours. Could've been us." Seven replied."Them pigs are fixin' to skin you alive, darkie, and I'm lookin' forward to watchin'. I think I hear 'em now." He said, looking over his shoulder, towards the direction of the wailing police sirens.

"That sirens I hear?" Boo asked, drawing near.

Without another word, Rusty swiftly clamped down as hard as he could on the teen's forearm.

"Ow!" Seven shouted, rubbing his arm. No sooner had he released his grasp on his pajamas, did Rusty take off running.

"Hey! Come back here!" Seven shouted after him. He and Boo took off running after the boy, but Rusty, running on pure adrenaline, was too quick.

CHAPTER SIX

With her thin wrinkled hands trembling, Margaret Browne touched her face. Her eyes were stretched wide in shock as she stared at her mahogany-colored hands, then at her reflection. Her hair was still an awful blue, but it sat on her head in a low tightly coiled afro.

"Lord." Was all she could say, although she kept her mouth open.

She had been standing there inside her bathroom for the past twenty minutes without an inkling of what she should do next. She had no one she could call. Her housekeeper, Charlene, was downstairs tidying up the living room and would be upstairs any minute to make the beds.

Mrs. Browne quickly wet one of the decorative scented Avon soaps she kept near the sink. She lathered up her hands, then scrubbed as if her life depended on it. When she rinsed the suds off and saw that her wrinkly hands were still the color of an acorn, she began whimpering.

"Jesus, Mary, and Joseph. What have I done to deserve this?" She whispered.

There was no way she could let anyone see her his way. She had too much pride to call her family physician or the sheriff's office.

Margaret Browne stared into her eyes, as she finally came to a decision. She could only think of one thing to do.

She walked out of the bathroom and stood at the top of the staircase. Making sure she could not be seen, she shouted for the housekeeper to leave for the day.

"But I haven't even started on the upstairs bedrooms." Charlene protested.

Mrs. Browne quickly assured her that it was okay. "You'll still get paid your ninety-five cents for a full day's of work tomorrow. Just git out."

She waited until she heard the back door open and shut before heading to the attic. She looked around a bit before finally finding what she was looking for.

"Forgive me, Lord." She whispered, heading back to her bedroom.

Continued in Black Out

ALSO BY THE AUTHOR:

KOKO: A NOVEL

PICK ME BLUES

BAIT & SWITCH

DESI EVER AFTER

QUEEN OF MEAN

KOREEN UNFILTERED

ALTER EGO

FED UP: TALES OF REVENGE

VIXEN

FOURSIGHT

BLACK OUT

DADDY'S GIRL

BEFORE THE BEGINNING

Thank You!

Thank you for your purchase! Please let me and others know what you thought about Negus by leaving a review on Goodreads or Amazon.

Be sure to connect with me on Instagram at @author.wenda for promotions, giveaways, and upcoming projects. I can also be reached at wendapromo@gmail.com.

Made in United States
North Haven, CT
14 June 2023

37753113R00090